The fog soon dropped again, but Hannah made no move to throttle back...

There it was! Hannah spun the wheel with all the strength of her good arm. Unable to brace herself with her other arm, which was in a sling, she lost her balance and nearly fell from her seat. The spray of a bright red paddle wheel trailing after a ghostly white steamboat left Hannah dripping.

Plainly, in gold letters along its side, was painted, *President Lincoln*. The steamboat let out a shrill blast from its whistle that almost made Hannah jump out of her skin. Then it vanished.

Other books in the

Hannah's
Island

S E R I E S

A Hound for Hannah
The Mystery of the Sunken Steamboat
The Mysterious Stranger

About The Author

Eric E. Wiggin was born on a farm in Albion, Maine in 1939. As a former Maine pastor, Yankee school-teacher, news reporter, and editor of a Maine–published Christian tabloid, Wiggin is intimately familiar with the Pine Tree State and her people. He has strived to model Hannah and Walt after courageous examples of the Maine Christian youth he knows well.

Wiggin's ancestors include Hannah Bradstreet Wiggin, and one of his four granddaughters is Hannah Snyder. But his greatest model for the *Hannah's Island* series is Hannah, mother of the Prophet Samuel, known for her faith and courage in adversity.

Wiggin's ten novels for youth and adults are set in rural or small-town Maine. The woods, fields, and pasture lanes of the Wiggin family farm sloping toward a vast Waldo County bog furnish a natural tapestry for the setting of many of his books.

Author Wiggin now lives in rural Fruitport, Michigan with his wife, Dorothy, and their youngest son, Bradstreet.

The Mystery of the Sunken Steamboat

Eric Wiggin

Emerald
Books

P.O. Box 635
Lynnwood, WA 98046

The Sunken Steamboat Mystery
Copyright © 1995
Eric E. Wiggin

All Rights Reserved.

ISBN 1-883002-25-7

Published by Emerald Books
P.O. Box 635
Lynnwood, Washington 98046

Printed in the United States of America.

Contents

Chapter One

Trapped!

"What do you suppose it is, Walt?" Hannah's voice betrayed excitement as the image shaped up on the sea green tube.

"It's huge, that's for sure." Walt adjusted the dials on the electronic sonar Papa had installed in his big Chris-Craft motorboat to help his tourist customers locate fish.

Hannah peered over her big brother's shoulder, watching the underwater shadowy mass take shape on the lighted screen.

"It...it *looks* like a sunken ship, like the pictures of the *Titanic*," she said in awe. Hannah held Hunter the Hound by his collar. Hunter was all aquiver with the excitement he caught from his mistress.

"No ship ever sank in Moosehead Lake," Walt disagreed. "This isn't the Atlantic Ocean."

Like Hannah, Walt had watched a TV documentary at Uncle Joe and Aunt Theresa's about the discovery of the famous *Titanic*.

"But there's that old schooner rotting in the mud cove back of Mt. Kineo," Hannah protested. "That's a ship."

"This here's three times as big as that schooner. It's got to be a big, natural underwater rock formation," Walt said importantly. "And if this drought continues, the water'll soon be low enough so folks'll hit it with their boats. I'll just tie a buoy to it, 'fore we head back to Beaver Island."

"I'm goin' down," Hannah cried. "Gimmie the rope."

She had tied her long, strawberry blonde hair back and slipped into her flippers while her brother was talking.

Walt was like that. He usually was nice. But being older—and a guy—he sometimes thought *he* should do all the really important stuff. Hannah and Hunter would have to wait in the boat.

But not this time.

"Hannah, that's *my* job," Walt protested, ignoring her request for the rope. "Besides, you're not wearing your swimsuit."

"So what? Anyway, my jeans are ready for the laundry."

Hannah snatched up the weighted end of the nylon rope coiled against the blaze orange styrofoam buoy resting in the bottom of Papa's boat. She grabbed her waterproof flashlight and dived overboard before Walt could complain again.

The steel weight on the end of the rope pulled Hannah rapidly downward toward the shadowy mass underwater, but Hannah wasn't worried. She and Walt had often taken turns diving for freshwater clams on the rocky bottom of the lake near the foot of Mt. Kineo. Hannah could hold her breath and descend at least twenty feet without Walt's diving gear, then surface, panting, but be ready to go back down after a few gulps of air. Hannah liked to dive without the bulky air tank if she planned to come right back up.

Hannah's waterproof flashlight cut a beam deep into the underwater gloom, lighting the huge, black mass. The object could be a big rock, sure enough, for along the lakeshore a number of great granite formations ran out of the forested hillside and disappeared underwater. Maybe Walt is right, she thought, as she played the light along, looking for the best place to anchor the buoy. She couldn't swim to the surface with the weight, so she'd have to decide quicly.

Hannah kicked with her flippers and followed the long, dark shape to its highest point. The buoy had to be tied to the shallowest spot if it was going to prevent boats from scraping against this bulky object.

Hannah swam to a tangle of waterweeds around a large object that seemed to be made of long slats and attached to the end of the black mass. A bar ran across this strange object. Now or never, Hannah told herself.

Hannah tried to loop the rope around the bar, which felt like steel, not soft like the rotten wood she had expected to find. But the bar was slimy, and Hannah's fingers slipped. In dismay, Hannah followed the weighted rope with her flashlight beam, watching it plummet deep into a black, underwater abyss.

Out of breath! Hannah realized she'd stayed too long, and she couldn't wait to untangle the weighted rope. Oh, well, she thought peevishly, kicking hard for the surface. Walt and I can grab the scuba gear and try again.

The surface seemed near enough, and though Hannah carried a heavy flashlight, her flippers pushed her quickly upward, and she was confident that she would soon pop up into the air.

Suddenly Hannah could go no farther. Something slick and wiry had coiled itself around her slender waist. She stopped swimming to fight the creature, which slithered tenaciously down, hungrily hugging her legs. Hannah felt as though her lungs would burst. She let go of her flashlight so that she could use both hands to fight back.

Down, down, down Hannah felt herself being dragged into the deep, black hole where she'd dropped the rope and weight, her flashlight somersaulting crazily into the darkness ahead of her as she was drawn toward certain death. She wanted to scream, but all she could do was expel the air from her lungs. The water—or whatever held her—seemed as though it would crush the life out of her.

Chapter Two

A
Secret Adventure

Thrashing and struggling beneath the cold water of the northern lake, a terrified Hannah fought frantically to free herself from the creature—whatever it was. The beast clawed and bit, sending up a shower of air bubbles that blurred Hannah's fading vision. Hannah felt herself being pulled roughly by the hair. Then she passed out.

"Help...me...sit...up." Hannah struggled and grabbed for Walt, who knelt beside her as she lay across a couple of boat cushions.

Walt straightened up. He held Hannah's shoulders as she coughed, retched, then coughed some more.

"I...I feel like I swallowed the whole lake," she wheezed at last. "Tastes like puke."

"You swallowed a lot of it. I had to give you mouth-to-mouth resuscitation."

Hannah coughed some more, then vomited.

"Ow-ooo," worried Hunter.

"Maybe we'd better head for Laketon and have a doctor check you over."

"Don't...*cough, cough, cough*...be silly. I'm...*cough*...goin' back after my flashlight with our diving gear."

"My diving gear," Walt corrected. "Uncle Joe and Aunt Theresa gave it to me for my birthday—remember?"

"Oh, yeah. Sor-ry!"

Hannah had stopped coughing and gagging, and now she struggled to rise from the boat bottom to sit on a bench. Her legs wobbled, and Walt caught her under her arms, helping her to a seat on the boat.

"I'm gonna be fine," she gasped at last. Glad as she was for Walt's help, Hannah was not one to admit she was sick so long as she could sit up. Hannah examined a rip in her jeans at the hip, and she patted it. Sore. She drew her fingers away.

"Blood!" she cried aloud. "It...it felt like I was being pulled under by an octopus and clawed at the same time—no wonder."

"That octopus was the rope and the weight. Hunter saved your life. I'm not surprised that he scratched you up a bit."

"Hunter pulled me out?" Hannah squealed, startled.

"Hunter dived right in and chewed the rope in half. Then I dragged you into the boat by your hair and arms."

"Oh?" Hannah felt her head, which was sore, too. "I guess Hunter clawed me in the process," she said, checking her bleeding hip again.

Hannah hugged her wet hound, kissing his cold nose. Then she slid down to one of the boat's cupboards for a bottle of peroxide from the first-aid kit. By the time she found it, Walt had strapped on his air tank and diving equipment.

"Going down to meet Davey Jones?" Hannah joked, swabbing her scratch with the disinfectant, then holding gauze against it to stop the bleeding. "I dropped the weight and my flashlight into a deep hole next to a bunch of slats attached to something circular. Definitely not a rock formation!"

"If we're lucky, your flashlight's still shining," Walt commented wryly. "Besides, I still want to tie that buoy to whatever is down there," he added, nodding toward the buoy, now drifting off toward the middle of the lake. "Sure you're all right, Sis?" Walt added.

"I'm fine...really." Hannah rose to her feet to prove her point.

Walt stepped overboard, and Hannah watched, concerned, as he submerged at once, bubbles rising as he dived toward where she had been trapped. She considered how moments earlier she had almost died down there. Could there be a water creature in there, not just the rope and Hunter like Walt said?

"I suppose there's nothing to worry about," Hannah shrugged. She peered over the side of the boat. Only a stream of air bubbles appeared, proving to Hannah that somewhere deep below the surface of Moosehead Lake her brother was still alive.

"I'm not scared. I won't get scared," Hannah said firmly, hugging her white, tan, and brown long-legged hound.

The sun had dried Hannah's tee shirt, and Hannah's legs had gotten their strength back by the time Walt surfaced. Only a sore throat from coughing up water reminded Hannah that she'd nearly drowned.

"It's a boat, all right," Walt shouted, grinning. In

one hand he held Hannah's flashlight, and the rope that Hunter had chewed off to free Hannah was draped across his fingers. "That thing you said looked like slats—it's a ship's paddle wheel. Boat's resting on its side, and you dropped your flashlight between the stern of the big boat and the paddle wheel. That's why it looked to you kinda like an underwater cave."

He grabbed the motorboat's ladder and started to climb aboard.

"What kind of boat?" Hannah asked.

"Tug."

"Tug?" Like that ol' boat at the dock in Laketon that's been made into a restaurant—the *Northland*?"

"Yep." Walt passed Hannah her waterproof light.

"But a tug wouldn't have a paddle wheel—those were on river steamboats!" Hannah protested. "'Sides, why would anyone bring a tug to Moosehead Lake? Tugboats are used in big city harbors, like in New York."

"Then there's the *Northland*," Walt chuckled, a little too smugly, Hannah thought.

"But the *Northland*'s a restaurant!"

"They didn't build a tugboat with big engines and everything just to feed a few tourists each summer. Think about it," Walt said, sounding like a typical guy, Hannah thought in disgust.

"I guess you're right. But why?"

"Remember that movie, *Maine Yesterday*? Uncle Joe has it on video. It showed a tug towing a huge raft of logs—remember?"

"I guess I didn't...you mean?" Hannah suddenly realized what Walt meant. "Was that the *Northland*? But the lake was full of logs!"

"Sure was," agreed Walt. "Until about thirty years ago, so I read in my history book, they used to tow logs to the paper mills with tugboats. And some of the older ones had steam engines and paddle wheels, like a Mississippi riverboat."

"So we've found an old tugboat, which nobody has salvaged 'cause they don't tow logs anymore?"

"Righto!" Walt was confident. "Now we've got a job to finish." He held up the chewed end of the rope. "Weighted end's tied to the paddle wheel," Walt explained. "We'll just leave Hunter here swimming, hitched to this end, while we go after the buoy that's floated off," he teased.

"We will NOT!" Hannah tossed her brother a life preserver cushion. "Here. This'll float. Tie the rope to it."

The styrofoam buoy had drifted about a quarter of a mile farther out from shore, and since Walt still had his air tank and flippers on, Hannah started the motorboat and opened the throttle. But the boat's wake pushed the float out of reach as they pulled up.

"Go get it, Hunter!" Hannah cried. She laughed in glee as Hunter plunged in and dog-paddled after the float, his long, brown ears streaming behind his head.

"That's his Labrador retriever blood at work," Hannah said proudly.

But try as he might, Hunter could not retrieve the floating buoy. It was simply too large and slippery for him to get his teeth around.

Walt had his tank and flippers off by now. Hannah stepped onto the prow of the motorboat, where she did a back flip before swimming out to Hunter. Hannah dived, planning to come up under the buoy.

Directly beneath her, farther down than the other, but near enough to the surface so she knew that she or Walt could reach it with the scuba mask and air tank, was *another* huge black mass. By now the sun was almost overhead, and Hannah could see the object outlined sharply against the sandy bottom of the lake. It was the front half of a ship, a long one, Hannah guessed from the size of the section that lay on the lake bottom!

"Papa will want to hear about *this*," Walt said importantly as they motored toward their home on Beaver Island after tying the buoy to the other wreck.

"It's two halves of the *same* wreck—it's gotta be," Hannah said in amazement. "And please, let's not tell Papa or Mama or *anybody* 'til we know for sure what we've found," she said, her face shining with pleasure. "It's a much larger ship than a tugboat, isn't it, Walt?"

"Sure looks like it." Walt ran his fingers through his sandy hair. "Y' know, it's goin' t' be kinda fun, us knowing about a shipwreck lying on the bottom of this big lake and nobody else knowing about it. Sorta like finding an ol' Spanish galleon loaded with pirate gold at the bottom of the Caribbean!"

Hannah hugged Hunter closer, trying to help her hound feel her excitement over the secret adventures she and Walt were anticipating.

Chapter Three

The Shipwreck Man

"I want to start my history research project tomorrow if we're goin' to Augusta, Mama," Hannah said one summer day.

The Maine state library was always one of Hannah's favorite places, crammed as it was with exciting books of all sorts about her beloved Pine Tree State. Hannah's favorites were the large, folio-size books of beautiful sailing vessels, their white sails tall against the wind. In olden days, Maine sailors sailed the seven seas and fought pirates and traded in the Far East, Hannah had read during trips to the library. Some captains long ago took their wives and children along, and Hannah liked to imagine herself climbing the ratlines with the sailors to hoist the sturdy canvas sails to catch the fresh breezes from off the open ocean.

Hannah remembered that she had once found a book in the library about the steamboats that used to bring freight and passengers up the Kennebec River to Central Maine from the sea. These ships were built like the riverboats of the lower Mississippi in the Old South, though they were smaller. As in the South, women in silk skirts twirled parasols or sat beneath a harvest moon as the grand sternwheelers and sidewheelers cut their stately wakes up the placid, black waters.

Hannah fairly burst with excitement as she thought about the secret she and Walt were keeping from Mama and Papa—a secret that she hoped to find a key to unlock in the library.

"I guess you're going to write a paper about ships," murmured Mama, never guessing that Hannah had a very special ship in mind.

"Sure am, Mama," Hannah giggled. I hope to learn enough to write a *book* about ships, Hannah thought. Well, a small book, anyway.

"Papa says you wrote a letter to the scientist who discovered the *Titanic* beneath the North Atlantic. It would really be an honor to get a letter from him, Hannah." Besides watching the TV special at Uncle Joe and Aunt Theresa's, Mama and Hannah had read in *National Geographic* about the scientist's exciting discoveries. "Has he answered?"

"No," replied Hannah sadly. "I guess he has more important people than me to think about."

"Any school student would be *proud* to have an interview with him to quote in a report," Mama chuckled.

"Since I'm home schooled, I guess there's nothing to be proud of," said Hannah thoughtfully, realizing that only her family would know about the interview. Truthfully, though, the very thought of talking with the great man, or even getting a letter from him, filled Hannah with secret pride. The *Titanic*, which had sunk in 1912 with nearly 1,500 passengers and crew, was considered one of the greatest sea tragedies of all time.

❋ ❋ ❋ ❋ ❋ ❋ ❋

The Maine state library, Hannah believed, was a marvelous place, quite unlike the Laketon public library, near her home. Hannah, however, felt quite at home there. On days when most other kids were in school, she could wander freely throughout the library's aisles and stacks, exploring marvels and wonders. Since she and her brother lived on an island and were educated at home, public libraries were their school library.

Mama or Papa or sometimes Uncle Joe and Aunt Theresa Boudreau took her and Walt to the state library at least twice during the school year. With each trip, Hannah would come home with an armload of books, which she returned by mail.

Hannah lingered at the museum displays in the hallway outside the library a little longer than usual today. A display of a ship's rigging was spread across real beach rocks decorated with artificial seaweed. A painted blue ocean scene portraying a clipper ship cutting the waves caught Hannah's attention and brought her thoughts back to her purpose for coming to the library.

Hannah hurried inside and went straight to the "Ships and Seafaring" section. Maine is an ocean state with two thousand miles of coastland. For four hundred years, vessels have been built in Maine to sail into every seaport on earth, Hannah had read.

Hannah thumbed through book after book in search of true tales of wrecked ships. She found several books about vessels on Maine's inland waters, but none about shipwrecks. These she laid aside. Finally, she settled on three volumes: One was a pictorial, with photos taken nearly a century and a half ago. It showed the passenger steamboats that had once steamed up her state's two great rivers, the Penobscot and the Kennebec.

The second book had stories of excursion steamboats on Sebago Lake, far downstate. In several nice old photos, women carried parasols as they rode the boat on their way to a picnic.

Another book, entirely about tugboats, had a beautiful, two-page color photo taken from an airplane. The photo showed Moosehead Lake ringed by gold and red maples in their autumn glory. A tug towed a huge raft of logs across the placid lake.

In the corner of the same photo, tucked away like a precious jewel in the blue water, sat Hannah's beloved Beaver Island. Hannah could just make out Beaver Lodge, smoke curling from its tall chimneys into the crisp fall air. Hannah snapped the book shut and kissed the cover. She added it to her pile to take home, without reading further.

Hannah fidgeted nervously as she waited in line at the library's checkout counter. Mama had left Papa and Walt at home on Beaver Island to tend to the guests. She had come to Augusta, the capital city, to visit the state office building to file papers for permits needed to expand their hotel, Beaver Lodge. Hannah had been alone for three hours in the library, and she had pulled down every book on lake steamships and riverboats she could find, flipping pages and looking at pictures. Where is Mama? Hannah wondered, as she stood in line.

The tall gentleman at the counter ahead of

Hannah took quite a while to check his only book out, and Hannah's three Atlas-size volumes were getting heavy. Hannah shifted her load from one arm to the other, which only made each foot tired in turn. Finally, she settled on propping the books on one hip.

The man seemed nice enough. He patiently produced half a dozen library cards—Hannah hadn't realized that a person could have more than one! The man fished out his driver's license and several credit cards for identification. The librarian frowned and studied them. Then she made a phone call, which seemed to take forever.

Finally, the librarian sighed. "This is *most* unusual, but your papers are all in order, sir. That's a rare book you're borrowing. It *must* be back in ten days," she added firmly.

"Sure," the man agreed pleasantly. He signed for the book, then stepped aside to cram his cards back into his wallet.

Hannah plunked her books on the counter. "Hannah Parmenter," she said with as much enthusiasm as she could muster, smartly slapping her library card down on her pile of books.

"I couldn't help overhearing your name," said the man, who seemed to have been waiting for Hannah while she checked her books out. "Are you from Beaver Island, in Moosehead Lake?"

"Y...yes, sir."

Mama had warned Hannah about talking to strangers. But this was a public library, not a dark alley.

Grinning broadly, the man reached out to shake Hannah's hand.

"Call me 'Professor.' And thank you for the fine

letter. Can I treat you to lunch at the Capitol Cafe? The rest of your family, too, if they're with you?"

"Wh...why, there's just Mama 'n me, today."

Hannah suddenly dropped her books. The professor at once bent to pick them up.

Just then Hannah spied Mama hurrying in through the library's double glass doors.

"Mama!" Hannah squealed. "This is the famous Shipwreck Man, and he wants to take us to lunch!"

Hannah at once felt every pair of eyes on the main floor of the library staring at her. The professor only stood there holding Hannah's books and smiled pleasantly.

Mama looked first at Hannah, then at the strange gentleman, then at the librarian. Her mouth opened and closed without any words coming out.

"He *is* a professor," the librarian said quietly, though uncertainly, as she tried to help Hannah out in her embarrassment. "From the Oceanographic Institute of Cape Cod, Massachusetts," she added. The librarian turned to the Shipwreck Man. "Are you the scientist who discovered the famous *Titanic*?" she inquired, the truth suddenly dawning on her.

"I'm afraid so," the famous scientist warmly answered.

"Well then," said Mama, shaking his hand, "we'll be your guests—I guess. Hannah's been dying to meet you."

"I had planned to phone you after my visit here to the library," the Shipwreck Man remarked pleasantly after he, Hannah, and Mama had ordered salads and sandwiches. "I considered calling you before I left to drive up here this morning, but it seemed too early," the professor added.

"I guess we came nearly as far as you did," Mama chuckled. "But who'd have thought we'd both be heading for the same library?"

Hannah's ears burned red. She was ashamed that only yesterday she'd told Mama she had decided that the important man was too busy to answer a plain country girl's letter. "I...I didn't ask much," Hannah stammered.

"You asked quite a bit, actually," he chuckled, tapping the old leather-bound book he had borrowed. "Like this book I borrowed for my own work, there's only a small amount of information available about ships in Moosehead Lake. But since I was coming to Augusta anyway, I looked some of it up for you."

"You found out all about the steamship on the bottom of Moosehead Lake!" Hannah blurted.

Mama raised an eyebrow, clearly puzzled.

"Am I giving a secret away?" the professor asked.

"N...not really. I mean, my brother Walt and I, we...we found something and we don't exactly want..." Hannah's voice trailed off. To tell the truth, she was uncertain what it was she didn't want.

"I understand perfectly," the professor said. "You would not believe the crowd of news reporters we had spying on us when we were working on the *Titanic* project. There were boats, helicopters, TV cameras, cameras with zoom lenses. And we were hundreds of miles from shore," he added in disgust.

" '*Titanic* was her name, Atlantic was her fame,' " Mama quoted the old song, joking.

"What did you find—about *my* ship, I mean?" Hannah could almost feel the great man slipping from her grasp before he would tell her what she needed to know.

"Well, since it's an assignment, I can't just tell you the answers, can I?" The Shipwreck Man winked at Mama. "And you won't find it in books," he added, nodding toward Hannah's pile of books.

"Then...then where?"

"Check your newspaper indexes about the hurricane of September 1938. Look for anything about the *President Lincoln*," he said mysteriously. "I've already found articles in the *Maine Sunday Telegram* and the *Bangor Daily News*. You can take it from there," he said.

"I *do* know how to look up newspaper articles—the librarian in Laketon, near where I live, taught me how. The old newspapers are all on microfilm," Hannah murmured, pleased. "Thank you, sir!"

"Sure. And you can use the library's equipment to make yourself photocopies to read later. That nice librarian will help you, I'm sure." The professor checked his watch and picked up the bill. "Got to scram. I need to do some research of my own, with the help of a print shop that can copy this antique book!" he added. "It's a long drive back to Cape Cod."

As they drove home, Hannah and Mama chatted for many miles about meeting the Shipwreck Man who had discovered both the famous *Titanic* and the *Luisitania*, sunk by a German submarine in 1915.

"Why were you gone so long, Mama?" Hannah asked at last. Without waiting for Mama's answer, she supplied her own. "I guess I'd never have met that famous scientist if you *hadn't* stayed away so long." Hannah was thoughtful as she continued. "I'm sure God knew just when I *really* needed for you to come back."

"You're right on that one." Mama patted Hannah's hand. "But to answer your question, the state inspectors say Papa can't build an addition to our small hotel unless he puts in an expensive new septic system. So I had to talk with a couple of bankers. It's going to be quite costly, I'm afraid."

"Yeah." Hannah slid down in her seat and said no more. She did not find such matters as sewers and septic tanks particularly interesting. Instead she pulled open a large manila envelope into which she had crammed photocopies of more than a dozen newspaper stories about the hurricane of 1938 and the sinking of an unusual sternwheel steamboat on Moosehead Lake. Hannah read these articles until she fell asleep in the car. To the hum of the tires on the highway she dreamed of finding old vessels with chests of gold beneath the waters of the northern wilderness lake that was her home.

Chapter Four

Pherson's Folly

Hannah turned Ebony onto her special trail from the pasture through the woods and up Bald Hill. Hunter was out of sight by now, baying his head off after a rabbit, but Hannah did not call him back. He could not get off Beaver Island anyway, and there were no deer for him to chase this time of year, so she knew he'd come home by nightfall.

Her horse reached a straight stretch of logging road crowded with young balsam firs. The road led along Juniper Bog, and the soil was soft and free of dangerous rocks. Hannah gave Ebony free rein and let him gallop. Her long, strawberry blonde hair flowed free in the breeze, and sitting bareback like an Indian queen, Hannah clung to her horse without stirrups or saddle.

Papa had promised to buy Hannah a saddle if he ever got far enough ahead of the bankers to have any spare cash. Hannah knew her parents had struggled since Papa had sold his half of a supermarket in Skowhegan and bought most of Beaver

Island on Moosehead Lake, with the old tourist lodge that needed constant repairs.

Now there was the trouble with the bankers. What had begun in bright hope with Papa's plans to expand Beaver Lodge and put in electric lights and a new sewer system had all turned sour. State inspectors demanded that Papa spend thousands more than the bank would loan. Only last evening Hannah had sat, chin in hands, on the hallway stairs landing listening as Mama and Papa discussed what they might do to pay the mortgage and save Beaver Lodge.

But Hannah would try to put these cares behind her for a while. Mama had given her the afternoon to herself. What better thing to do than become queen of your own island world for a few hours!

Hannah turned Ebony onto the path winding up the hill. It was her own private, special path she had created as part of a trail that led to secret places only she knew about. At one point, Hannah had created a long detour that zigzagged through a cedar thicket, rather than bring Walt or Papa up here to help her move rocks with a crowbar to make a straighter path.

Presently, girl and steed emerged from the woods into an open blueberry barren. Ebony was walking now, but Hannah urged him to a canter as the slope tapered off, until at last they were at the island's highest point.

Slipping off her panting stallion, Hannah tethered Ebony to a gnarled birch growing crooked beside a boulder. She climbed atop the rock and sat cross-legged for some moments, watching motorboats cutting long wakes across Moosehead far below. Here and there a flash of spray showed a water skier making a power turn on the big blue lake. How grand Hannah felt up here where, merely by turning around, she could view her entire world and the world beyond.

Hannah peered closer in, to where Beaver Lodge's copper roof shimmered in the afternoon sunlight. How pretty Papa's small, grey-shingled barn appeared way down below. The barn was set like a jewel amongst the green of the fields and pasture, with Molly the brown Jersey milk cow and Bullet the beef steer munching their red sweet clover and switching flies with their tails.

What better place to be in all the world? Hannah pondered sadly. Was all this beauty, this island, this marvelous world to be torn from her before she could even finish growing up?

Her mind reeled backwards a few years to an auction that she, Walt, and her parents had attended at a dairy farm near Skowhegan. A man in their church had injured his back. Unable to continue his farm work, he had to sell everything—barn, cows, machinery—even the house and its furnishings. One of the man's daughters, Tessa, had been Hannah's dear friend, and they had hugged each other and sobbed as her family saw its possessions hauled off in pickup trucks and U-Haul trailers, often sold at less than value to the greedy auction crowd.

Papa had bought for Mama the washing machine that had been Tessa's mom's. He had privately given Tessa's mother fifty dollars more than the auction price. "Vultures!" Papa had remarked about the auction crowd as he drove his family home, angry at seeing his friends treated so.

Was Hannah's family now about to lose everything, too?

Hannah peered again toward Beaver Lodge. A brand-new wing that would contain four bedrooms, each with its own bath, was partly finished. The timbers were bare, for the crew of carpenters had days earlier packed their tools and gone home. Piles of dirt and ugly ditches showed where the state health inspector had made the plumbers quit work before the new sewer lines could be finished.

Now the bankers in Augusta threatened to foreclose, despite having talked so confidently with Mama the day she and Hannah had met the Shipwreck Professor at the state library. They now refused to loan Papa the extra money needed to meet the state inspector's demands.

To make things even harder for the Parmenters, the tourist business had been off during the summer because of rainy weather—the same rainy weather that had kept Hannah and Walt from visiting the old shipwreck.

"The bankers have given us ninety days," Papa fretted. "But unless I can finish those extra rooms, there is no way I can pay the bank back." But the whole family knew that only the bank could furnish money to pay the carpenters to finish the rooms.

"They've got us in a corner," said Papa.

"What about the Lord?" Mama had quietly asked. "He owns the cattle on a thousand hills, and He knows all about our troubles."

Mama was like that. She'd worry over little things, like running out of cooking gas just before several guests were to arrive. But when Papa got down, Mama lifted him up.

God is like that, Hannah thought. He gave me parents who never get discouraged at the same time.

Hannah gazed again at the clear blue lake, thinking of what she and Walt had discovered way out toward Mt. Kineo. But for weeks the weather had been too miserable for scuba diving.

Hannah thought about her Heavenly Father for a few moments. She had been reading from the book of Genesis, chapter 16, and she had been enraptured by the story of Hagar, the Egyptian slave. Expecting a baby and alone in the wilderness, Hagar had murmured, "Thou God seest me," as in faith she became aware of God's special care for her. Hagar believed that the God who knew all her troubles would provide for her. God did—when Hagar obeyed God and went home.

Like Hagar, I am alone, with only a hound and a horse for company, Hannah mused. "You God, You do see me," Hannah repeated Hagar's prayer, believing it would be answered for her also. At once Hannah felt an urge to discover what lay in the ruins of that old boat beneath the lake.

Hannah whistled, and she was surprised to find Hunter already beside the boulder where she lay. "Let's go, fellers!" Hunter knew what that meant, and he stood obediently, letting Hannah use him for a step stool to mount Ebony without stirrups.

Hannah went straight to her room after the supper dishes were washed. She yanked a manila file folder from her bureau drawer and spread its contents on the bed. The folder was stuffed with photocopies of old newspaper articles and pages of books about the old days of steamboating on Maine rivers and lakes.

What fascinated Hannah most was an article entitled "Captain Pherson's Folly." The article told how Civil War General Elihu Pherson had made a fortune in shipbuilding after the war. About one hundred years ago he had retired and bought an old steamboat from the Mississippi River, the *President Lincoln*, which had a twin, the *General Grant.*

Captain Pherson had sailed his grand stern-wheeler to Maine, then up the Kennebec River as far as Augusta. Here he was stopped by a mill dam. He hired a crew to cut the ship into two pieces, load it onto railroad flatcars, and ship it to Laketon, where it was bolted back together and steamed across Moosehead Lake.

Hannah laid down the article. Catching her breath, she peered past her window curtains to Papa's wharf. Had the *President Lincoln* ever docked at Beaver Island? she wondered, enthralled.

She again took up the photocopied article, studying every detail of a photo of the old steamboat. The photo showed a long, wooden-hulled vessel, a stern-wheeler with a huge paddle wheel behind. Was this the same wheel where she'd dropped her flashlight and nearly drowned, where even now Walt's buoy bobbed to warn boaters? she wondered. But Hannah and Walt had both decided that the paddle wheel belonged to a tugboat. It can't be, Hannah thought.

The ship had three decks with railings all around and two tall stacks belching black coal smoke. A crowd of passengers—women in long dresses, men in straw boaters—waved gaily from the top deck as the *President Lincoln* steamed away from the dock in Laketon.

The article told how not enough tourists would come far north to Moosehead Lake to make the big steamboat profitable as an excursion boat. The captain lost money season after season. Captain

Pherson died in 1921, a ruined old man, and his steamboat was left by his widow to rot at the municipal dock in Laketon.

That was a long time ago, Hannah thought. I suppose there's nothing left of it, she sadly decided.

Hannah flipped a page, and a very small news clipping fell out. It had been stuck to the back of another sheet. The clipping was from the *Bangor Daily News*, dated September 21, 1938. "*Lincoln Sinks*" was the short heading. Hannah had photocopied every article she could find about the hurricane of '38, as the professor had suggested. Here was one she and Walt had failed to read:

> On the night of Sept. 19, during the height of the hurricane, an abandoned excursion boat drifted away from its mooring at the Laketon dock. The ship, locally known as *Pherson's Folly*, was brought to Maine some forty years ago by retired Capt. Elihu Pherson. It is believed to be a former Mississippi River steamboat, the *President Lincoln*. The huge, rotting hulk evidently sank in the night, out of sight of human eyes, on the north side of Moosehead Lake. This was a great relief to town officials, who have wondered for years how to dispose of it.

One paragraph. That was all. Somehow Hannah believed that the *President Lincoln* would rise in all its glory once again. And she was determined to have a part in its rising!

Chapter Five

There's Got to Be Gold!

Walt stopped milking Molly to hear what Hannah had to say. "Gotta hurry," he grumbled. "Papa's asked me to go to Laketon in his big motorboat to buy supplies this morning."

Some of Papa's worries had begun to rub off on Walt, Hannah fretted. It was not like Walt to be grumpy, she thought, remembering that Walt had been grumpy quite a lot before God changed his heart.

"Walt, is your scuba diving gear ready to use?" Hannah began.

"Sure. But money's tight. Papa's not going to let us burn up his gas in the motorboats."

"He'll let us go diving if we buy the gas, won't he?"

"I suppose. Ask *him*, okay!" Walt started tugging at Molly's udder again.

"Walt?" Hannah didn't wish to upset her brother. But she had to ask.

Her brother looked up. "Yeah?"

33

"What I really need to know is, if I buy the gas, will you go diving with me at that old wreck?"

"I suppose."

It sounded to Hannah like Walt was making a promise he didn't expect to keep.

"This afternoon—really, truly promise me. 'Cause I'm buyin' the gas."

Walt sighed. "Awright. I'll go."

An elated Hannah headed for the house.

"Hey, Sis," Walt's voice came from the barn. "I really *would* like to explore that old wreck with y'."

After breakfast, Papa took down his Bible for family devotions. "My God shall supply all your need according to his riches in glory by Christ Jesus," he read from Philippians chapter 4. Papa reminded the family that that meant that God would supply *in the same measure as* God is rich, as we have need.

After Papa's reassuring words, Walt left for Laketon and Hannah set to work helping Mama with the housework. By mid-morning Mama excused her, and Hannah set off to find Papa where she'd heard him pounding and sawing on the new wing of the lodge.

Hannah held a ten-dollar bill up to Papa when he put his hammer down. "Papa, I...."

"Hold it," he interrupted, "we can't take you kids' savings."

"I don't mean that, Papa. Walt and I want to use one of the boats to go scuba diving this afternoon. He thought you'd let us if we paid for the gas."

"Something about a sunken tugboat? Last time you and Walt were out there, we nearly lost you. I just don't know."

"Yes, Papa. But it's more than that." Hannah smiled primly.

"Oh?"

"A secret."

"Well, I guess I shouldn't refuse a secret. But I have got to insist on inspecting the wreck before I let you go back down. Walt says it's an old log-hauling tugboat."

"We're not sure, Papa," Hannah truthfully admitted. "It's in two big pieces, about a quarter of a mile apart."

At once Hannah feared she'd said too much. Her and Walt's secret was slipping away from her. She had determined to learn all she could about the sunken ship before telling anyone about it.

"Tell you what," said Papa, checking his watch. "I don't have time for a lot of diving. But if you and Walt can take me over this afternoon to where Walt's tied that buoy, I'll do a safety inspection. Just *don't* go crawling inside a sunken ship, okay?"

"We won't, Papa," Hannah promised.

"Papa, why are you working on the lodge, if the bank's cut off our money?" Hannah asked, changing the subject. She didn't wish to talk about her special secret anymore.

Papa pointed to piles of boards and shingles.

"Those building supplies will be worth more than twice as much if I assemble them in the shape of a building," Papa chuckled. "I don't know what the Lord's going to do for our family, but I'm sure He'll bless us if we trust Him and I do my best with what He's already given us."

"And He's given *me* some direction, too," Hannah firmly put in. Hannah was not ready to tell Papa yet, but somehow, she felt, the Lord might use that old sunken ship to help her family.

❋ ❋ ❋ ❋ ❋ ❋ ❋

"Looks okay to me," said Papa as he popped out of the water. "I'd agree with Walt that it's an old tug." Papa clambered into the boat with Hannah and Walt and began to unstrap the scuba tank. "You said you got tangled in the buoy rope, not the wreck itself, right?"

"Yes, Papa. That's what happened."

"I don't suppose it's likely to happen again. Freak accident," Papa said slowly. Hannah could tell he was worried.

"Where are you and Walt going to start diving?"

"Out there." Hannah pointed to an orange buoy, about a quarter of a mile farther out.

"It's lying right on a sandy bottom, Papa," said Walt. "There's nothing for us to get tangled up in."

"Well, okay." Papa checked his watch. "Watch your depth—and be careful!" He stepped across the gunnels into the other motorboat. "Be home in time for supper." Papa started the motor and roared away.

Walt had placed a second buoy on the other part of the wreck, and he and Hannah were soon anchored above it.

"Shall we send Hunter down first, to see if there's an octopus or a shark?"

Before Hannah could stop him, her brother had thrown her hound overboard. To their delight, Hunter found it sport, and he paddled off to the buoy and tried to bite it. When he found it too big for his mouth, Hunter paddled back so that Hannah could haul him aboard.

"Now it's my turn," Hannah cried, seizing the scuba tank. Walt helped her strap it on, and she leaped in at once.

God had provided several days of blue skies

without rain. The water was clear, though much deeper than in early summer, when a nearly snowless winter had left Moosehead dangerously shallow. Hannah kicked with her flippers, pushing herself across the hulk below as she played her flashlight back and forth.

This ship was evidently much longer than the tugboat *Northland*, for each half was nearly as long as the floating restaurant tied up at the Laketon dock, though about the same width. It had several decks with railings, like in the news photo. But only gaping holes were left where the tall metal smokestacks had once stood.

Hannah swam past both sides of the stern, hoping to find the ship's name painted on the hull. Any painted name, however, had peeled off and dissolved many long years ago. This section of the ship had the wheelhouse, and Hannah decided to look there. At the very top, next to its flat roof, Hannah found a brass plaque, so green with corrosion that even if it were above water, it could not be read, Hannah decided. *Probably so corroded we'll never know what it says,* Hannah thought as she pushed for the surface to give Walt a turn at exploring the wreck.

"I've got an idea," Walt said when Hannah told him about the corroded brass plaque. He fished a screwdriver out of the boat's tool kit, then tied it to a length of nylon rope, leaving several feet of the rope loose beyond the screwdriver. "Give me time to get down there, sis, then lower this where you see my bubbles coming up." Walt grinned slyly. "I really think you've got something with that news clipping about the sinking of that old steamboat."

Walt had been underwater perhaps ten minutes

when he tugged the rope for Hannah to haul it up. The brass plaque was heavy, and more than two feet long. When she got it to the surface, Hannah found she could not lift it over the side of the boat. "Uh-h-h-n-n-nn!" she grunted.

Hunter grabbed the rope with his teeth and began to haul with his mistress.

With Hunter on the rope, Hannah let go and grabbed the plaque, which she feared would slip from Walt's knot. Then she felt it being pushed upward. Walt had surfaced, and he grabbed the boat's gunnel with one hand as he pushed with the other. The plaque soon clattered into the boat.

"What is it, Walt?" Hannah cried, looking at the long, corroded piece of metal. She turned it over. One side was lumpy, like there might be raised letters under all that slime and corrosion.

Walt began to dig at the scaly stuff with his pocketknife. Hannah grabbed the screwdriver and set to work at the other end. She soon found a small letter *n*. Walt found a capital *P*.

They stared at each other. Without speaking, they both began to chip away near the middle of the plaque. Walt uncovered a small *t*. This was followed by a capital *L*, which Hannah found. She could see that the words might be, *P———t L——n.*

"We've found it!" Walt cried.

"The *President Lincoln*!" squealed Hannah, hugging Walt with all her might. "Gimmie the scuba gear. I'm going back down!"

Then brother and sister laughed together watching Hunter, who was scratching away at the plaque with his claws.

Hannah soon popped back to the surface. "Walt," she cried, "can you swim to the bottom without the air tank?"

"Sure. Can't stay down long, though."

"Follow me!" Hannah dived again. She took Walt to a brass-bound chest that seemed to have fallen from the *President Lincoln* when the steamboat broke in two. It was half buried in sand and locked with a heavy, old-fashioned padlock. In the minute or so before Walt ran out of wind, he and Hannah tugged hard several times, but they could not budge the old chest.

"'Sixteen men on a dead man's chest,'" sang Walt as topside, he helped Hannah out of the scuba gear.

"Walt, you've been reading pirate stories again!" Hannah protested.

"Yup. That's from Robert Louis Stevenson's famous book *Treasure Island*," Walt admitted. "And you know what, sis? That chest is *exactly* like the treasure chest on the book cover. Do you suppose...?"

"I don't suppose," Hannah softly answered. "But I can pray. Mama and Papa are going to lose Beaver Lodge to the bankers if somebody doesn't find some money real quick. There's *got* to be gold in that chest, Walt," Hannah insisted.

Chapter Six

Walt Has a Plan

"We can raise that chest with Papa's big boat and the old block and tackle hanging in the barn—you know, that thing with the rope and pulleys on it," Walt shouted over the roar of the motorboat as they headed for Beaver Island. He had been thinking a mile a minute, like Mama sometimes said. Walt was finally getting excited over the shipwreck discovery.

"But we have to get it loose from the lake bottom first," Hannah protested. "And with only one scuba-diving outfit, one of us is going to have to work alone."

Hannah was sure she couldn't do the job by herself. Somehow, she didn't think Walt could do it alone, either. Besides, Hannah had found the chest, and she wanted very much to help dig it out.

"I'm pretty sure I could cut the padlock off with Papa's hacksaw."

"Underwater? Don't you *dare* try that!" Hannah protested. "We'll spill whatever's in it all over the lake bottom." Hannah had just read a *Reader's Digest* article about a crew of treasure hunters who had found the steamship *S. S. Central America* sunk in the Atlantic Ocean after 130 years. Its cargo of California gold was scattered across ten acres under the sea. Hannah was not about to let that happen to *her* treasure—not when she had read that old gold double eagles could be worth $30,000 apiece!

In her heart, though, Hannah realized it was unlikely they would find gold in Captain Pherson's old trunk—not very much, at least.

"Then why don't we just *rent* another scuba outfit from the Laketon Village Rentals?" Walt suggested. "We can get one for twenty bucks a day, I think."

"'Cause you've got t' be 18, or they won't let you have it, that's why," Hannah mourned. She could see her secret being let out before she was ready, when she had to ask Papa to sign rental papers for a scuba outfit.

"Tell you what," said Walt, not defeated. "Mama'll want me t' take the boat to Laketon tomorrow to get the mail. I can just ask Uncle Joe to sign. He'll keep a secret. Can you afford half the rental for a scuba outfit?"

"Sure can," Hannah brightened. She did not tell Walt that the ten dollar bill Papa had refused to take was all the money she had in the world.

That evening, Walt rigged a long boom from old boards and a heavy fence rail. He hid them under Papa's dock so that he and Hannah could use them later with the block and tackle to haul the chest from the lake.

"Let's go to the barn, sis. And bring your flashlight," Walt said after supper, with a mysterious wink at Hannah.

"Molly's not about to have her calf?" Mama asked, surprised.

"Heavens, no," Papa said. "The calf won't be along for a month yet."

"Well, I haven't seen those kids so excited about anything in *weeks*," Mama fretted.

"I expect it's got something to do with their aquanautic endeavors out by that old sunken tugboat," chuckled Papa. "They think they're Navy frogmen," he teased.

"Frog *girl*," corrected Hannah. "An' I won't turn into a princess if you kiss me, either."

Papa kissed her anyway.

"See. Didn't work." Hannah grabbed her flashlight and danced out the door after Walt.

Walt was already on the high-ceilinged barn floor eyeing the block and tackle when Hannah arrived. "Just what we need," he said. "It's about as high from that beam where it's hanging down to here, as the water over that chest is deep."

Hannah pointed a beam of light up into the shadows and frowned. "Somebody's got to go up there and unhitch it. Papa's ladder isn't long enough, I'm sure."

"It'll come down same's it went up," Walt said importantly. His masculine engineering ability was coming out.

"How's that?"

"Shinny up and wriggle out onto the beam." Walt pointed to a wooden brace angling up from the haymow.

Hannah could see that anyone could get up to the brace by stacking up a few hay bales.

"I'll pile some hay underneath in case you fall."
Walt began moving bales of hay toward the middle
of the barn.

"In case I fall?"

"I'm not going up there," Walt said defensively.

"Chicken!" Hannah put her hands on her hips
and glared at Walt.

"Am not!"

"You're afraid of heights!"

"I get dizzy when I climb."

Hannah's mind ran back to when she and Walt
were little. Big brother Walt had screamed his crazy
head off when Hannah'd climbed to the top of the
apple tree in their backyard in Skowhegan. But by
the time Mama had came running to rescue her,
four-year-old Hannah was already back playing in
the sand box. Maybe some people can't climb,
Hannah pondered. But Walt could sure dive. So she
said no more.

But skidding sideways on a beam too narrow to
crawl on is a bit more exciting than climbing an
apple tree, Hannah soon discovered. The wood was
rough, which made it easy to grab onto. But
Hannah kept getting splinters whenever she sat
down. Walt's yelling, "Don't look down!" didn't help,
either.

Hannah finally reached the tackle. It took a
powerful lift with her slender fingers, but she eventually got it unhooked while hanging on for her life
with her other hand.

"Walt, get that block and tackle off those hay
bales!"

Walt grabbed the ropes and pulleys and stepped
back, surprised.

Without another word, Hannah grabbed the

beam with both hands and swung off, monkey-fashion.

"What are you doing?" Walt bellowed. "Tryin' to kill yourself?"

Hannah let go and dropped, sailing free. She landed, then scrambled off the hay bales, trotting quickly to the open barn door to examine her hands in the light of the setting sun. Her worst injury was a handful of splinters from swinging around the rough beam.

Chapter Seven

The Secret Is Out

Everything moves in slow motion underwater. Being just about weightless doesn't help, either, when you're trying to dig for treasure, Hannah and Walt soon discovered. Walt had brought two shovels and a heavy crowbar, hoping that he and Hannah could dig for a while, then pry the chest loose.

They could dig okay—except that the water made it impossible to throw a shovelful of sand very far. When Walt pried down on the crowbar, he zoomed up. Hannah grabbed the crowbar along with Walt, and they both shot toward the surface as soon as they pushed down.

So they had to dig clear under the chest. Finally, they got a rope under it. Walt swam to the surface and began to pull. Hannah stayed with the big trunk to steady it as it went up.

She was surprised at how light the big box seemed once it came out of the hole. But Hannah remembered smashing her toes on some underwater rocks near Papa's dock. When she had moved them so it wouldn't happen again, she found they were easy to lift, until she tried to lift them above the water. Papa had explained that any object under water weighs less in proportion to the amount of water it displaces.

Sure enough. As soon as the chest broke the surface, it became so heavy that Hannah and Walt couldn't get it into the boat. Walt grabbed Papa's hacksaw.

"*Not yet!*" Hannah screamed. "Not until we get it to land." They lashed the chest to the boat. They couldn't travel fast, but they got along okay with Walt hanging onto the chest and Hannah driving the boat.

"*Mama!*" Hannah yelled half an hour later. "*Come see!*" Hannah and Walt now had the chest dragged onto the rocky beach in front of Beaver Lodge where Walt had cut the padlock at once. Hannah suddenly forgot that they had a secret. The cat, as Mama would say, was out of the bag.

Mama was as startled as Hannah when she looked into the chest. Though the straw packing had rotted long years earlier, Hannah's treasure was as bright and beautiful in the sunlight as when it had been new.

Walt and Papa prepared supper for the guests that evening while Mama and Hannah unpacked the treasure on a porch table. There it was—blue willow pattern table service for twenty-four, and not a piece scratched, chipped, or broken! Oddly, though, one cup and one saucer were missing.

"What's it worth, Papa?" Hannah cried, her eyes shining as Papa came onto the porch for a look.

"A few hundred dollars, at least. Hm-m-m-mm."
He picked up a dinner plate. Like all the others,

it had a Southern plantation mansion in the center, with "Arlington House" written underneath and the initials, "R.E.L."

"Looks like some kind of commemorative issue of china," Papa observed. "The Arlington House is in the National Cemetery outside Washington, D.C. I'd say old Captain Pherson bought these three sets when the cemetery was dedicated in 1883," said Papa, who is a history buff. "They probably made thousands of them. Its value to an antique dealer will depend on how many are left."

"It's all *one large set*," said Mama, who had counted the serving dishes.

Hannah was crestfallen. She had hoped for treasure enough to pay the bankers off. "A few hundred dollars" surely wouldn't do that.

"Y...you an' Mama can use the money to pay the bank," Hannah said quietly, sadly. "Perhaps it will help a little."

Papa patted Hannah's head. "The money will go into your college fund, sweetheart. I'm going to Augusta next week. I'll have it appraised then. Better pack it away."

The next morning, when Hannah took the motorboat to Laketon to return the scuba gear Walt had rented, she took along a saucer of the Pherson china. The public library, Hannah knew, had some books on antiques. Perhaps she could find this set listed and get an idea of its value.

"Your china was fired thirty years *before* the Arlington National Cemetery was founded."

Old Miss Farnsworth, the retired librarian, was substitute librarian on the regular librarian's day off. And she *knew* all about this china set!

Hannah's head swam with this news.

Miss Farnsworth was as old as Moosehead Lake itself, or so it seemed to Hannah. Nearly ninety, she enjoyed good health and a quick mind. Though she had retired twenty years ago, she still worked in the library several days a month, so Hannah had met her a couple of times. Miss Farnsworth knew every detail of local history—"She's forgotten more than the others know all put together," said Aunt Theresa Boudreau one day.

"Did you ever see our library's Pherson scrapbook?" Miss Farnsworth asked.

"No." Hannah was excited and a little embarrassed. She had read everything she could find on her own in the Laketon library about Captain Pherson and his ship. She figured confidently that she knew about as much as anybody about the old captain. Now Miss Farnsworth was to prove her wrong. Hannah had once asked the regular librarian about the *President Lincoln*, but she could only talk about rumors and knew nothing of any other written accounts.

Miss Farnsworth produced a small, old-fashioned key with an odd, round shaft. "Follow me." She scanned the small library's one reading room, and the only patron was a man asleep under a newspaper.

"Oh." Miss Farnsworth stopped suddenly in front of a glass case on the wall. It contained two very old china dolls. "These are the Pherson dolls. Given to our library by Mrs. Pherson herself, 'fore she died," Miss Farnsworth chuckled. "Old Cap'n was rumored to have mebbe a dozen more, but they were never found. Went down with his steamboat, most likely."

Hannah got goosebumps at this revelation. She

peered closely at the dolls, then at a silver tag on the case. It was so badly tarnished that you could read it only if you already had an idea what the words were. It said, "Gift of Elihu Pherson Family." Wow, Hannah thought silently. I never *knew* that, though I've seen those dolls many times.

The old woman trotted down a narrow hall to a musty room filled with boxed back issues of magazines. A wooden box about as deep as a shoe box but three times as wide sat on a shelf in the corner. Miss Farnsworth tried unsuccessfully with shaky fingers to insert the key.

"You try it, dearie," she asked.

Miss Farnsworth made no move to remove the key from the leather thong that tied it to her belt, so Hannah had to crowd in front of her to unlock the box. "I keep the only key t' this box—never let it out o' my sight," Miss Farnsworth explained.

Miss Farnsworth extracted a leather-bound scrapbook brimming with news clippings and photos. She turned pages for what seemed to Hannah like hours. Now and again with gnarled fingers, she would hold a clipping, read some of it aloud, then put it back.

"Here we are," she said at last. From the scrapbook Miss Farnsworth produced several old pages from *The Saturday Evening Post* dated September 24, 1951. "The Mystery of the Lee China" was the title of the article.

The article featured a color photo of a single cup and saucer that matched Hannah's set exactly. The initials R.E.L. fairly leaped at Hannah from the picture. *Robert E. Lee*, the famous Civil War Confederate general! This thought shot through Hannah's brain like an electric current. Hannah was shaking visibly now, worse than the ninety-year-old librarian.

"C...can I make a copy of that article?" Hannah squeaked, remembering the photocopy machine by the checkout desk.

"Why surely, dearie." Miss Farnsworth answered as easily as if she permitted folks to copy the article every day.

That evening Hannah, Papa, Mama, and Walt each read the article. It told how General Lee had carried a cup and saucer in his saddlebag all during the Civil War. His mansion, the Arlington House, had been raided by Union soldiers, and most of its furnishings were taken as booty of war.

When the mansion was restored as a public museum, the rest of the china could not be found. It was traced to a former Union Army general, Elihu Pherson, the *Post* writer said. But Captain Pherson had died in 1921, and most of his possessions had been sold by his widow to pay debts.

Most exciting of all, the Arlington House china was one of a kind. It had been specially commissioned by General Robert E. Lee himself before the Civil War. No duplicates or extra pieces of the twenty-four place setting had ever been made.

"We're millionaires," Hannah murmured that evening, awestruck.

"Our chickens haven't hatched yet," Papa admonished. "Probably not a million dollars, but I'd guess it's worth a few...quite a few thousand, Lord willing."

Right after the china was sold at an auction in New York, Papa paid the bankers, bringing the mortgage up to date. He also used only enough of the money needed to finish the sewer, and the bank loaned him enough to finish the new wing on Beaver Lodge. "It's not right that I should use my children's money to build my own business," Papa said.

"But Beaver Lodge will be ours someday, anyway," Hannah laughed. Papa insisted, though, that most of the money be put into trust for Walt's and Hannah's college education.

Chapter Eight

Two Men From Missouri

"Wow!" shouted Walt.

"Let's see it!" Hannah cried, grabbing at the *Bangor Daily News* Papa had bought in Laketon. Hannah had been washing dishes, and she snatched the newspaper away from her brother without drying her hands. Papa only grinned and held up a dozen photocopies of the front-page article he'd already copied for friends.

Laketon Girl Finds Rare Lee China, said the headline, two columns wide near the bottom of the page. The photo with it showed Hannah standing with R. Carleton Reynolds, III, a rich philanthropist. Mr. Reynolds, the article said, had purchased the rare china set at a New York auction for "an undisclosed sum." Then he had given the china to the Arlington House in the National Cemetery to make its set complete.

Most of the article, Hannah noticed indignantly after she'd read a couple of lines, was about Mr. Reynolds' work in helping famous museums.

"Papa, what's 'AP?' " Hannah asked, pointing to the letters in parentheses next to "New York," just under the headline.

"That means Associated Press. They're the ones who took your picture after the auction and asked you a few questions, remember?"

Hannah did not remember. So many exciting things had happened to her family in New York that she was still trying to sort them out.

"The Associated Press sends those articles to every daily newspaper in the country. Many of them will publish it," explained Mama, who had once taken a journalism class in college.

"That means Hannah's famous," said Walt, who had quietly read a photocopy after Hannah had rudely ripped the newspaper from his hands, tearing the front page in half.

"It takes more than that to become famous, I'm afraid," Papa mildly remarked.

"Like being a rich philanthropist who gives important gifts to museums," Hannah grumbled. To tell the truth, she was angry that Mr. Reynolds was given more credit than she, who had found the china. Hannah seemed unconcerned, however, that Walt, who had helped her rescue the chest of china, was not even mentioned.

"Maybe that," Mama chuckled. "Rich philanthropists do get a lot of attention."

The new cellular phone Hannah had bought for the family buzzed.

"I'll get it," Papa sighed. "When we had to use the CB radio and have Uncle Joe patch us through to phone calls, we didn't get bothered by calls nearly so much."

"And until we got this phone, we missed a lot of

calls that would have given us business," Mama said pertly, as she hurried off to make her Beaver Lodge hotel guests comfortable.

"Long distance for a Miss Hannah Parmenter—anybody here by that name?" Papa cried a moment later.

"Bob Parrish, here, from St. Louis," Hannah heard on the phone. The man had a pleasant voice, and he sounded as old as Papa. But he had an accent that reminded Hannah of a country and western singer, only not as nasal. "I saw y'all on TV with that philanthropist," Mr. Parrish said.

Mr. Parrish explained that he and a business partner, Harry Duke, had started to restore an old steamboat, the *General Grant*. They planned to use the *General Grant* for excursion runs on the Mississippi River from St. Louis to New Orleans several times a year.

Then Mr. Parrish said something Hannah did not understand. His ship, the *General Grant*, had been built more than one hundred years ago using the same blueprints as Hannah and Walt's *President Lincoln*. He and Mr. Duke wanted to come to Maine to explore the wreck of the *Lincoln* and perhaps salvage some parts of it to use in rebuilding the *Grant*. Then Mr. Parrish asked to speak to Papa.

"Can you and Walt give two nice Southern gentlemen a tour of your underwater steamboat?" Papa asked Hannah after he had chatted awhile with Mr. Parrish.

"Sure can, Papa!" Hannah cried, her spirits lifting.

Papa talked a bit more. "We'll see you fellows next week, then. And we'll save the best rooms in the house for you and your partner," Papa said. Then he hung up.

"Papa, what did Mr. Parrish mean about the blueprints?"

Papa pointed to a chart he had tacked to the bulletin board in the kitchen. "That's a blueprint."

"But Papa," Hannah protested, "that's the *plan* for the new addition to Beaver Lodge."

"A plan like that is called a blueprint," Papa explained, "Because it's printed on blue paper or with blue ink."

"I guess ships are built with plans, too," said Hannah. "Did Mr. Parrish mean that he's *found* the plans for the *President Lincoln*?"

"No," Papa said patiently. "Only that he's learned that the exact same plans were used to build his ship as to build yours. So when the ships were new, they were identical."

"It's as if Papa's blueprint has been used to build a hotel addition somewhere else," Walt said, his mechanical mind racing ahead.

"And it *has*," Papa said. "There's a tourist home in Skowhegan with a wing exactly like the one the carpenters are building for us. I liked it so much when I saw it that I had one just like it built here. By using the same blueprints, I saved more than a thousand dollars."

"But if the blueprints to the *President Lincoln* are lost...? I don't get it," Hannah protested.

"The *steamboats* are exactly the same—that's the important thing," said Papa.

"Oh!" Hannah brightened. "Then parts from *our* steamboat will fit theirs!"

"You got it," Walt agreed. Walt knew that his sister was sharper than he in history, so he didn't tease her about not catching on about mechanical things as quickly.

❋ ❋ ❋ ❋ ❋ ❋ ❋

"We're excited about the boat y'all found down there."

Mama poured Mr. Parrish another glass of iced tea.

"Yes," agreed Mr. Duke, "the boiler, engine, connecting rods—they're all intact. Don't seem t' rust as fast in these here cold northern lakes as they do da-own South. We can use the engine for sure," he drawled.

"But the *President Lincoln's* broken right in half," Hannah protested.

"Our thanks go to old Cap'n Pherson," said Mr. Parrish. "It's broken right where he cut it in half to load it onto a freight train, so it didn't do much damage. Ah b'lieve it could be bolted right back t'gether, could we raise it."

"We might could do that, come winter," Mr. Duke said. "Yew folks hev such thick ice up here—strong enough to support a crane, Ah've heard."

"Sure do," Walt agreed, pleased that the Southern gentleman had taken note of one of his state's well-known natural resources.

"Wait a minute," said Hannah. "That's *our* boat!"

"What Ah'm proposin'," replied Mr. Parrish, "is that y'all get to keep all the artifacts not actually a part of the steam boat. If there's a ton of gold in there—but of course there isn't—it's all yours. You already have the china, for example. Any trunks, boxes, pieces of furniture, tools—stuff like that we may find—is yours, and we'll even salvage it for you, as much as possible. All we're interested in is the boat itself, with its engines. We need them to restore our steamboat in St. Louis. Fair enough?"

"What happened to the *General Grant's* steam engines?" Papa asked.

"They were sold for scrap metal many years ago," explained Mr. Parrish. "Nobody ever dreamed that steamboat travel would become popular again. But the *President Lincoln's* engines have been protected from scrap metal raiders by about twenty feet of water. And since both steamboats were built following the same blueprints, the *Lincoln's* boilers and engines will fit the *Grant* perfectly."

"Won't they be ruined after sixty years underwater?" Hannah was puzzled.

Mr. Parrish picked up the bronze plaque from the *President Lincoln*, which Hannah and Walt had proudly showed him and Mr. Duke. The heavy plaque was shiny and nearly new looking as he placed it across his knees. "When you found this, it was so badly corroded you couldn't even read it, you said."

"Yes," agreed Walt. "I took it to a machine shop in Laketon and had the corrosion sandblasted off."

"Exactly," the Southern businessman said. "The *Lincoln's* engines will have to be sandblasted to clean them up. Some parts will have to be cast from new metal. But, you see, you can't restore an old part unless you *have* an old part to restore."

Chapter Nine

Dolls by the Dozen

Several weeks later, Hannah recalled Mr. Parrish's remark about having to have an old part to restore an old part. Mr. Parrish and Mr. Duke hired a barge with a crane to anchor above the wreck of the *President Lincoln*. They hired divers to help the crane operator bring up the *Lincoln's* engines, winches, and other mechanical parts of which the *Grant* had been robbed during its long sleep on a muddy bank of the Mississippi. As the men promised, everything they found not actually a part of the boat they turned over to Hannah and Walt.

Brother and sister were rapidly collecting many small antiques and personal items—silver knives, forks, and spoons, glassware, several pieces of jewelry, even some old mirrors with ornate bronze frames.

Each afternoon after the divers and crane crew went home to Laketon or Skowhegan, Hannah and Walt would take Papa's motorboat out to dive for

58

perhaps an hour. Hannah found genuine ivory combs, mother-of-pearl buttons, brooches, coins, and silver buckles that the divers, who were looking for steamboat parts, had passed up. But it was the middle of September, and Moosehead Lake was getting chilly. Pretty soon Hannah and Walk would have to quit, though the professional divers might continue to dive wearing wet suits until the lake froze over.

"Let's go diving, Walt," Hannah said one Saturday morning. Sunday was the first of October, and a thick layer of frost had covered the porch railing that morning when she went to the barn to take her turn at milking Molly.

"Too cold, sis. We'll freeze."

"You can stay in the boat. I'll go down."

Hannah believed it would be spring before she saw the *President Lincoln* again, and she wanted to explore her wreck one last time.

"You're crazy. You'll die of hypothermia," said Walt.

Hannah said no more for the moment. She ran to the lake, took off her sneakers, and, hiking her jeans above her knees, she waded in. Walt was right. Hannah tried to imagine what it would be like to jump into water *this* cold all over. Then she had an idea.

Hannah ran to the kitchen of Beaver Lodge. Mama won't mind, she told herself as she fished a half-full can of shortening from the cupboard. Secretly, Hannah was glad Mama was not there to ask questions. She went straight to her room, where she found her swimsuit stretched on a hanger to dry. Hannah had read about the brave woman who had first swum the English Channel in the ice-cold

North Atlantic. She had greased herself with lard to keep the frigid water out of her skin's pores as she swam all day in one of the world's coldest bodies of water.

Covered with shortening from her toes to her ears, Hannah slipped into her swimsuit. She chuckled, thinking that for once the suit wouldn't stick to her skin when she took it off. Then Hannah pulled her jeans and an old sweatshirt on over the mess.

"C'mon, Walt," she said, slipping downstairs on greasy feet.

Walt silently surveyed the grease on his sister's hands and face for a moment. "Latest thing in make-up?" he asked at last. "Isn't it supposed to be green?"

"You're just lucky you're my favorite brother or I'd pound you," Hannah said. "Are you going with me or not?"

"Suit yourself," Walt shrugged. "But you'll be screaming for me to pull you in soon's you get your feet wet."

Hannah decided that the greasing she had given herself with shortening really did help as she plunged into the icy water. Later, when Mama scolded her for "risking your life and health by jumping into a nearly frozen lake," Papa calmly remarked that "from a strictly scientific point of view, Hannah had a good idea."

To Hannah's surprise, after the first shock of cold, her body quickly adjusted to the icy lake. Hannah had decided to explore only the rear half of the steamboat, wanting to see how it looked with the paddle wheels removed. The wheels had been pulled aside and left on the lake bottom when the divers hauled the big steam engines out.

Hannah kicked with her flippers, peering with her waterproof flashlight into the huge hole left by the engines and boiler. The crew, she discovered, had set the old wreck upright with their crane while working on it.

What is this? Hannah pushed herself down to the lake bottom to examine an old wooden box on which a decking plank was resting. She pushed the plank out of the way easily enough, then gave the box a shove. The box rolled right over and appeared to be fairly light.

Since the box was not stuck in the mud, Hannah guessed that it had fallen from the wreckage when the engines were pulled out. But the box had hinges and a padlock! Whatever was in it Captain Pherson had considered valuable enough to protect with a lock.

Hannah picked the box up. She could lift it underwater, but she couldn't swim to the surface with it. No way. The nylon rope Papa always kept in the boat soon solved that problem.

Even with her sweatshirt on, Hannah nearly froze as Walt motored toward Beaver Island with the box tied onto the boat.

"You're going to be sick." Mama was worried when she saw Hannah shaking and trembling from the cold. Hannah was not sick, however, and a hot shower quickly warmed her up and washed the shortening off. But the minute that Hannah was finished in the bathroom, Mamma snapped, "You go straight to bed, young lady." Clearly, Mama was more concerned for Hannah's health than Hannah was.

Maybe Mama was right, Hannah thought when she awoke. It was late afternoon, and she had slept for four hours! Swimming in ice water sure tires a girl out, she decided. And it leaves her hungry, too.

But what is this? Hannah was startled when she followed her nose into the kitchen where Mama was making supper for guests who had come to see the fall colors. While Hannah was sleeping, Papa had built a rack of chicken wire, which he had placed behind the wood-fired kitchen range where Mama was baking a pot of yelloweye beans.

"Look what was in your box," Mama said, smiling. She was in a better mood, now, which greatly relieved Hannah. "Count 'em," Mama said.

Miss Farnsworth at the library had been right. Here were twelve china dolls! Their bodies were sodden with lake water, and their clothes, though all there, were stained and ruined. But each doll had a perfect head, two perfect porcelain hands, and perfect feet.

"We can make new doll bodies from cloth and sawdust, like the old ones," Mama explained. "When they're dry, we can even make them new clothes, using the old dresses for patterns."

Hannah decided at once to give her dolls feminine versions of the names of Jesus' twelve apostles. She found the apostles' names in Luke 6:13-16. Here are the names that Hannah gave to her twelve dolls:

Petie, Andrea, Jamie, Johanna, Phyllis, Bertie, Mattie, Thomasina, Jimmie, Simonetta, Judy, and Judith Iscariot.

Chapter Ten

Hannah's Business Venture

"It's not fair...," Hannah said one October afternoon as she and Mama were sewing dresses for the twelve apostle dolls. Hannah bit her tongue and did not finished her sentence. Instead, she eyed her fine antique china dolls sitting in a row on a shelf in Mama's sewing room. Though they were all exactly the same size, which made stitching their cloth-and-sawdust bodies much easier, each doll had a different face. Hannah had learned from Miss Farnsworth at the library that during a trip to China, Captain Pherson had carefully selected as many fine examples of Chinese dollmaking as he could find. He had purchased fourteen, all different, and twelve of these were now Hannah's.

Hannah thought for a moment about the lesson in having twelve dolls with such individual personalities. Then she considered how to reword her sentence so as not to get a lecture from Mama. The last time Hannah had said that something wasn't fair, she'd heard from Mama about how God has made us all different and how He has given each of us an individual personality and has put us all in different circumstances for our benefit and blessing. "Helen Keller, Louis Braille, and Fanny Crosby were blind, for instance," Mama had pointed out. "The Lord permitted this so that they might better use their other senses to make others happy and glorify the Lord," Mama had added.

You couldn't argue with Mama on that one, Hannah admitted. Mama was right, too, when she said that the most frequent complaint heard from kids is, "It's not fair!" Hannah heard this complaint often on the several days she spent in school each quarter to take her tests and get some special help. The rest of the time, Hannah and Walt were home-schooled by their parents on Beaver Island.

Hannah felt her conscience cut like a knife when she remembered Mama's words for this kind of grumbling: "It's blaming God." Right now Mama was waiting for Hannah to finish her sentence. Hannah decided to turn into something positive what she really believed to be entirely negative.

"I could earn money every week if Walt and I could dive down to the shipwreck and gather stuff the salvagers miss," Hannah proposed. That was positive, though maybe a little far-fetched.

"I'm sure you could," Mama agreed. "But the last time you dived you nearly froze to death—remember?"

"Isn't that stretching things a bit, Mama? I was cold, sure, but hardly near death."

Hannah looked up from cutting paisley silk with pinking shears for Mama to stitch. Far down the lake, Hannah could see the salvagers' boat bobbing at anchor above the sunken *President Lincoln*. On the lake bottom, she knew, two men in wet suits were busy removing brass hardware and nickel-plated plumbing fixtures to replace equipment lost from the *General Grant*. In another six weeks, Hannah realized, Moosehead Lake would be covered with ice. Most of the stuff that she wanted to rescue would need to wait until next summer.

"The antique dealer paid me more'n a hundred dollars for that shoe box of mother-of-pearl buttons and silver buckles," Hannah said. Mama had taken a negative approach to what could easily become an argument. Hannah was determined to stick to the positive side.

"That's great, honey." Mama knew this was money Hannah could spend for things for herself. The money from the Lee chinaware, however, had to remain in the bank.

"I can buy clothes with it, right?"

"Of course."

"Then I propose a business deal. Walt 'n I will buy ourselves wet suits for cold-water diving. Wet suits *are* clothes. They'll pay for themselves and make us money, too."

"I think," said Mama, "that you and Papa should talk before you and Walt go off on any wild-goose chases."

Hannah smiled silently. Papa had an adventurous heart like her own.

Several pieces of old tableware—solid silver—a couple of pewter mugs, a solid brass kerosene lamp, and an ivory brooch. These were the items that Hannah and Walt had to offer the dealer at Olde North Antiques. Papa said they could sell them to buy wet suits and spend perhaps a hundred dollars.

Papa set strict rules to be sure the diving was done safely. Never was either Hannah or Walt to dive without the other suited up and ready to rescue. And no diving in rough weather.

Papa privately told Mama that he didn't think the kids would go diving more than a time or two. But lessons learned that way are learned best, he said.

Hannah was soon disappointed with her enterprise. She learned that though a wet suit helps hold body heat, it does not really keep one warm. And there were no more chests of rare china or antique dolls to be found. Here and there a coin, a piece of whalebone scrimshaw, an odd cup or saucer, worthless old shoes—that was about it.

"We're bringing up more junk for Mr. Parrish and Mr. Duke than for ourselves," growled Walt one day as he eyed the collection in the bottom of Papa's motorboat. Walt and Hannah had found heavy iron bolts and fancy brass fittings that the two men from St. Louis would use to restore the *General Grant*. But they had found only a few things for themselves, mostly cracked or chipped pottery.

"We've sold just seventeen dollars worth of stuff since we bought these wet suits," Hannah mourned one evening at mealtime.

"I knew it wouldn't pay," said Mama.

Hannah glared at Mama but said nothing. Mama, of course, could not have known whether the enterprise would work until it had been tried.

"I'm sorry, honey," Mama apologized, seeing the hurt in her daughter's eyes. "I guess you still have several weeks of diving weather."

"What we need is a faster system to bring what we find back up to the boat," Walt put in. But neither he nor Papa had any suggestions.

Chapter Eleven

Hunter the Seal

"C'mon, boy," Walt called to Hunter. Walt clapped his face mask on and jumped from the boat. His Labrador retriever instincts taking over, Hunter sailed over the side of the boat into the icy lake after Walt. "Let's see if you can dive."

Walt flipped onto his back, keeping his face just above water. He let Hunter crawl onto his chest, then submerged, hugging Hunter gently.

Hunter, out of air, soon struggled to get free, and Walt let Hannah's hound go at once. Walt repeated this until Hunter had learned that Walt did not wish to drown him.

"Hannah, let's have your air tank with just the hose—no mask."

"It won't work with a dog, silly," Hannah protested. To tell the truth, she was tired of Walt's playing around when she wanted to get on with diving and treasure hunting.

"It worked in *That's Incredible*," Walt argued, referring to a TV show he'd seen at Uncle Joe's about a dog that could scuba dive. "May I at least *try?*" Walt sounded like Hannah now—persistent and a little unreasonable.

"Guess it won't hurt anything."

Hannah removed the face mask from the air tube, then passed her tank over the side of the boat to Walt.

Walt went into his act with Hunter, swimming on his back with the hound on his chest. Only this time, he thrust the air hose into Hunter's mouth just before he submerged.

Hannah watched the bubbles in concern, then checked her watch. Hunter had not stayed underwater more than thirty seconds before. This time he stayed a minute and a half.

❀ ❀ ❀ ❀ ❀ ❀ ❀

Sunday after church, the Parmenter family had dinner with Aunt Theresa and Uncle Joe Boudreau.

"I have to show you folks ze video I made on our trip to ze ocean this past summer," said Uncle Joe, as Hannah and her family were eating Aunt Theresa's delicious raspberry pie. Uncle Joe's Canadian French colored his speech when he was excited.

Hannah rolled her eyes at Walt, who smirked. Uncle Joe's travelogues were not their favorite Sunday afternoon entertainment.

"You've heard of ze *André* movie, about a seal?" asked Uncle Joe. The way he pronounced "André" made it sound as though the seal were French.

"Yes," admitted Mama. Even though the Parmenter family had only recently had Beaver Lodge wired for electricity to use with Papa's new generator, they had steadfastly refused to buy a TV set.

"It's a time waster," Mama had said.

"You can learn more from books," Papa had agreed.

But the weekend edition of the *Bangor Daily News* brought Hannah's family glimpses of the world beyond Beaver Island. From it they had learned that Maine's famous seal André had been put into a movie starring a silly California sea lion as André. The Hollywood filmmakers had cleverly included a few scenes from the real André's home village, Rockport, Maine. Everyone in Maine knew about André, according to Uncle Joe.

"I've got ze real André on video," said Uncle Joe as he popped a cassette into his VCR.

Hannah, who, like Walt, did not care for Uncle Joe's home movies, thought that Uncle Joe sounded very pleased with himself.

That night Hannah dreamed of André. In her dream, the seal was brown, white, and tan. He had odd, floppy ears that drifted behind when he swam. And he had a tail. Partway through Hannah's dream, André's flippers became hound-dog legs.

Hannah awoke the next morning with a perfect plan all worked out. She found an old waterproof poncho in the back hall and began snipping with Mama's sewing scissors. Using waterproof glue, Hannah added an old pair of snorkeling goggles she'd used before Walt got his scuba gear.

"Oo-o-o-o-oo," Hunter complained every time Hannah pulled this strange headgear onto his seal-shaped head. If Walt was going to teach Hunter to dive, she'd make the most of it.

The sewing room door popped open. "I've been

looking all over for that dumb dog," complained Walt, stepping inside. "Mama won't want him in *here*."

Walt held up an old propane gas tank that Papa had once used on his soldering torch. He had equipped the tank with a pressure gauge and a rubber hose. Using large hose clamps, he had attached two old leather belts. "Compressed air from Papa's tank," he explained.

"What y' got there?" Hannah asked, rolling her eyes. Walt was all the time making stuff, then throwing it away when it didn't work as expected.

"Tell me what *you're* makin' first," Walt demanded. He grinned as he watched Hannah fit the mask onto Hunter's pointed face as the hound struggled to get away.

"I can't believe it!"

"Can't believe what?" Hannah still did not realize what Walt had made.

"That we're *both* rigging a scuba outfit for Hunter."

Suddenly it dawned on Hannah that Walt's contraption would fit perfectly with the rubberized cloth waterproof mask she'd made.

"Walt, you're a dear," Hannah exclaimed. Then she did something she hadn't done since she and Walt were little kids. She kissed her brother's cheek and gave him a bear hug.

If Hannah could have laughed underwater, she'd have done a belly buster. But all she could do was grin through her mask as she watched Hunter the seal test his homemade flippers, fashioned from the soles of Hannah's outgrown sneakers. Hunter swam rapidly on the surface, plunging underwater whenever Hannah dived, then quickly surfacing for air. Hunter's ears streamed along behind him, just like Hannah had seen in her dream.

Hannah remembered that both American and Russian space explorers had taken dogs on space trips as canine astronauts. Would anybody really believe that she had taught a hound to be an aquanaut? she wondered.

Hannah was working at the lake bottom beside the wreck of the *President Lincoln*. Papa had fitted an old galvanized pail that had rusted through the bottom with coarse screen. This let lake water run through but kept safe anything Hannah found underwater that she put into it.

Hannah and Walt had been collecting small steamboat treasures by lifting the bucket to the boat by a rope. But the process was slow. The rope kept getting tangled in the wreckage, and often the person on the lake bottom would not be directly underneath the motorboat, so whoever was in the boat had to figure out where the other one was and keep rowing around. It seemed to take forever to get the bucket back down to the bottom.

Walt therefore had fixed another bucket like the one Papa had rigged. He fastened it to the belt around Hunter's chest with a brass snap hook. Poor Hunter! Though he kicked along at a good speed on the surface, and even seemed to use Walt's homemade aqualung to keep his head underwater, the extra weight terrified him. Instead of sinking gently, he spit his breathing tube out and began to claw. He lost both flippers, and had not Walt been able to rescue him at once, he surely would have drowned.

"You're just a plain ol' hound, aren't you boy," Hannah comforted, hugging her trembling dog. "No seal in you at all. A little Lab, maybe, but you're sure not an underwater animal."

Hannah discovered that the divers hired by her friends from St. Louis to strip the boat of usable parts were careless about saving things they did not need themselves. One day Hannah found on the deck of the *President Lincoln* an old pair of wire-rimmed glasses, the lenses crushed and broken. Something heavy had been dragged across them, and they appeared to have been ruined. In disgust, she tossed them into the bucket with some other junk, then hurried to gather a few more odds and ends, since it was about time to go home.

"You have something valuable here," Mama said that evening. She had been working on the old glasses with some tableware polish after carefully picking out the broken lenses with tweezers. Mama also found that she could straighten the nose pieces by careful twisting with needle-nose pliers. The frames themselves were not bent.

"Let's see." Hannah held the glasses up to a high-intensity lamp. Then she gasped. "Mama, it's...."

"Real gold," Mama finished Hannah's sentence. "The first you've found."

"Well, you kids have learned a valuable lesson in running a business," Papa remarked after the gold frames were sold for a good price to an antique dealer.

"I agree," Hannah said quietly.

After paying for motorboat gas and the cost of the wet suits, Walt and Hannah found themselves with almost exactly the same amount of cash on hand as when they started.

"We didn't make any money, but the fun was worth every minute," said Hannah. "I'd have really liked to have taught Hunter to dive, though," she laughed.

"That's the breaks," Walt chuckled. "Hunters hunt; Andrés dive. We want our dog to stay alive."

Chapter Twelve

Hijinks on
the High Seas

"Them fancy Southern dudes in patent leather shoes is stealin' our heritage," snarled the man across the counter from Hannah and Papa. Hannah had gone to Laketon that morning with Papa, who had left his snowmobile motor at a repair shop for servicing to get ready for winter. When Papa learned that they had to wait a couple of hours, he and Hannah stepped into the Pine Tree Cafe for hamburgers and some pie.

Hannah's ears pricked up at the word *Southern*, since her friends Mr. Parrish and Mr. Duke were from St. Louis. If you live in Maine, that's a long way down South, indeed. Hannah eyed the fellow who had spoken. The man was rough and unshaven, and he wore greasy hunting clothes with tears and holes—not the nice new stuff that Mama and Papa's guests at Beaver Lodge wore during hunting season.

Papa ignored the man's crude talk.

Hannah shot a second glance at the fellow, who

74

she realized was staring at her. Since her picture had been in several newspapers following the sale of the Lee china, Hannah was no longer surprised when total strangers spoke to her or just looked. How thankful she was for Beaver Island, where she never met curious eyes or nosy folks wanting to know how much she had been paid!

"Ain't you supposed t' be in school t'day, sweetheart?" the man remarked in a low voice.

Is he speaking to me? Hannah looked around, but she was the only kid in the restaurant.

Papa's eyes narrowed as he also decided that the comment was meant for Hannah. "She's with me, Burt," Papa told the man. Papa's voice was pleasant, but the expression on his face said, "Don't mess with us."

"That was Burt Buker," Papa said as soon as they left the Pine Tree Cafe. "If he'd get himself a job, he wouldn't have so much time to nose about in other people's affairs."

"Did he recognize me?"

"'Fraid so."

Papa said no more, and Hannah was much happier when an hour later the motorboat was headed full throttle for Beaver Island. Papa was at the wheel, giving Hannah some time to peer down the lake at where the salvage crew had anchored their barge. For more than a week now, the crew had left the front section of the *President Lincoln*—which could be seen from Beaver Lodge—and moved to the rear section, out of sight behind a wooded point. This week was to be their last salvage attempt. When Hannah and Walt had checked on them, the divers had said that they needed only a few gears and pulleys to complete the *General Grant*.

Hannah grew angry as she recalled how Mr. Buker in the cafe had ridiculed the way her friends were dressed. Mr. Parrish and Mr. Duke were businessmen from a big city. Did Burt Buker really expect businessmen to dress like woodchoppers or farmers? she wondered.

Is there really more treasure in the shipwreck of the *President Lincoln*? Hannah mused, as she laid her copy of *Treasure Island* on her nightstand and turned off the light. She shuddered when she recalled how R. L. Stevenson's fictional treasure had cost a lot of fictional lives. Late at night, when Hannah was tired, she had no difficulty imagining these murderous hijinks in the high seas happening right here on Moosehead Lake.

Even real treasure hunts, like the one on Oak Island, Nova Scotia, Canada, had cost a lot of people great sums of money with little to show for it, Hannah had read. Does God *really* want His people to spend their time hunting treasure? she pondered. Hannah remembered Solomon's lesson: He had asked for wisdom first, and God had given him treasure. As she fell asleep, Hannah prayed that the Lord might give her wisdom.

Yet something seemed to say deep within Hannah that the *President Lincoln* might yield one more treasure. This thought tumbled through Hannah's brain as she tossed and turned, dreaming of chests of gold at the bottom of the sea.

"Let's take one more dive before the big lake freezes over, sis." It was Walt speaking early Saturday afternoon. He had just returned from Laketon. The small lakes had already frozen clear across, Walt had learned.

"I'm game," Hannah chuckled. "How 'bout you, Hunter? Want t' freeze y' long ears off?"

"Better take blankets to wrap yourselves in," Mama cautioned. "And be sure Hunter gets wrapped up as soon as he shakes the water out of his coat."

Hannah and Walt were not surprised to find a boat tied to one of the No Trespassing buoys above the shipwreck when they rounded the point. The salvage crew had placed these floating signs here to keep curious onlookers out of the way. But Hannah and Walt both knew that the signs were largely ignored once the salvage crew returned to Laketon each evening.

"Not much to steal, anyway," Walt chuckled, "now that we and your friends from St. Louis have picked the wreck clean as a turkey bone."

Two men in wet suits climbed into an old cabin cruiser just as Hannah and Walt pulled up to the buoys. They glared at the brother and sister. "Get out of here!" one of the men yelled. He seemed to be swearing, but Hannah could not hear what he said, for his buddy started the boat's motor at that moment.

Walt laughed aloud as the fellow, a short, wiry, angry man, fell on his face when the other intruder opened the throttle.

"Walt, that's Burt Buker," Hannah said in dismay.

"Like I'm afraid o' him? He's all hot air," Walt growled.

Walt had seen Mr. Buker in Laketon and decided he was a coward and a bully. Walt just clapped his face mask in place and jumped in the water.

Hannah was worried, but she quickly strapped a new pair of homemade flippers onto Hunter and forgot about Buker and his buddy. She laughed as she watched her hound waddle awkwardly to the side of the boat, then plunge overboard and paddle off, enjoying what probably would be his last swim of the season.

Suddenly Hannah's motorboat trembled and rocked, as if it were being shaken by an unseen hand. Hannah sat down, hanging on as the water seemed to boil like Mama's soup kettle around her. The mud roiled up, turning the water black. There was so much splashing that Hannah could no longer tell where Walt's bubbles were surfacing. Hunter had disappeared in the water. Then all went quiet.

Quiet, that is, except that Hannah suddenly realized that Burt Buker and his sidekick were bearing down on her fast in their old boat. They pulled alongside, then Buker and his pal both leaped aboard Papa's motorboat. Buker grabbed Hannah by the hair and arm. She fought and clawed as he dragged her into his boat.

"Scuttle their boat, Lem," Buker commanded.

Lem carried an axe, which he swung over his head.

"Don't!" screamed Hannah.

Buker threw Hannah on her back, then he put his knee on her chest. Pain shot through her body as she felt a rib snap. The attacker dragged Hannah to a sitting position and pinned her arms behind her, tying her wrists with twine. The pain from the broken rib was so great now that Hannah could at first only gasp.

Hannah's eyes grew wide in horror as Lem stepped back into Buker's boat. Papa's boat had a gaping hole, and it was sinking fast as water geysered up.

And where were Walt and Hunter?

* * * * * * *

Walt struggled to get his leg free, but it was pinned to the bottom of the lake beneath the wreckage. What happened? The rear half of the *President Lincoln* had suddenly shifted, tumbling onto Walt just as he reached the bottom.

Something nudged his arm, then his cheek. Walt swatted it away. Pesky fish. I'm trapped. Now I'm catfish bait. Glad it's not the ocean—at least there aren't any sharks.

Boiling mud had blackened the water so that Walt couldn't even see his waterproof watch. Why couldn't this have happened out by the front half, where the bottom is clean sand? he asked himself.

The pest was back, nuzzling Walt's arm underwater. Walt reached again to push the creature away, but his hand struck a hairy body. It was Hunter!

Good boy! How Walt wished he could tell Hunter to go for help. Out of air, Hunter shot for the surface. Papa's going t' be mad, Walt thought. He told us to be careful.

Walt would have laughed at the silliness of his thoughts, but the seriousness of his condition again began to crowd in on him. I'm about to die, he thought. And Hannah's up there with no idea what's going on. Hurry. Go tell Hannah to get help before I run out of air! Walt screamed silently at the surfacing dog.

Hunter soon swam back down.

Walt pushed him off again, and Hunter surfaced once more.

Again, Hunter dived and swam back, determined to help his trapped friend.

Walt had an idea. Grabbing Hunter's collar, he held Hunter underwater until the hound began to struggle and claw. This time Hunter, nearly out of air, swam straight for the boat above them.

※ ※ ※ ※ ※ ※ ※

"Please help my brother. He's going to drown down there," Hannah begged.

"So let him," Buker sneered. "We didn't ask you kids to interfere with our little fireworks display."

"Fireworks?"

"Yep. Underwater dynamite. That steamboat your fancy city pals has been tryin' to salvage is history. An' we can't hev no witnesses."

I'm a witness, Hannah thought. Aloud she asked, "What are you going to do with me?"

"Drown you, I most imagine. Then it'll look like an accident."

God had given Hannah strength, and she felt no fear. "Then just drown *me*. But please call the fire department to rescue Walt before he runs out of air," she begged.

"The girl's right, Burt," Lem agreed. "I went along to blow up the old steamboat. I didn't plan on no murder."

"All right," Burt Buker snorted. "You just knock her out with an oar. I'll take care of the rest."

Lem picked up the oar. "Can't do it, Burt." Lem's voice trembled as he spoke.

Buker pulled a long knife from a sheaf in his wet suit.

"You come near me with that knife, and I'll brain you with this oar!" screamed Lem.

Something surfaced next to where Hannah sat.

She shot a glance at Buker, but his back was turned. Had Lem decided to help her? She decided to chance it.

Hannah arched her back to reach into the water behind her with her hands still tied, gritting her teeth to keep from crying out in pain. She felt a collar on a furry body. It was Hunter, gasping and coughing.

Hannah hauled with all her might, flipping her hound into the boat. "Sic 'im!" she gasped as she felt herself faint from the pain of the broken rib.

Hunter had Burt Buker's leg before he could turn around. "Crack!" Lem knocked Buker out cold with the oar.

"This boat has a CB radio," Lem told Hannah, cutting her bonds with Buker's knife. "Call the Laketon Fire Department! I'm going down to see if I can help your brother." He pulled his mask down and dived overboard.

Hannah dropped the mike as soon as the radio dispatcher promised her that help was on the way. Though her broken rib hurt terribly, she squeezed Hunter, helping him cough up water. "You saved my life, boy," she cried. "I only wish you could tell me if Walt is all right."

Chapter Thirteen

A Mystery Steamboat

"You bundle up real good—and keep your speed down."

"Yes, Mama."

Mama should know by now that I'm almost grown up, thought Hannah. Besides, Hannah prided herself that she was the only kid her age on Moosehead Lake with a State of Maine boating safety certificate. But somehow Mama always seemed to remember the foggy morning Hannah almost rammed a bull moose with the motorboat as he grazed in shallow water.

This was one of those November mornings when the season's change brought pea soup fog to the damp hollows and lakes of the northern woodland. Mama had insisted that Hannah wait until nine o'clock, then ten. Finally at a quarter past eleven, Mama decided that the lake fog had lifted enough for safe boating.

"I trust you as much as I do myself," Mama said.

Yeah, sure, Hannah thought. Parents never trust their kids until they're at least 18.

"I'll be careful, Mama," Hannah promised for the umpteenth time.

"Run the fog lights. And honk the horn every hundred yards or so, whether you see anyone or not," Mama admonished.

"I'll drive with one hand on the horn button," Hannah promised tartly. With a broken rib from the thrashing she received from Burt Buker, blowing the horn was about all her left hand could do.

In just a few days, the Parmenter family would be cut off from the outside world for perhaps a month. Thin late-fall ice would rip the hull of any boat put into the lake, sinking it quickly, and it would take several weeks for the ice to become thick enough to support a snowmobile. Only if a Maine Forest Service helicopter would land on Beaver Island could Hannah's family be rescued in an emergency.

But November was a busy month at Beaver Lodge. Deer hunters came from all over, and Papa worked as a full-time guide for out-of-staters, taking them in one of his boats to the best spots along Moosehead's north shore for hunting. So Papa's other boat had to make daily trips to Laketon, not only to supply the hunting guests but also to prepare for a month of isolation, which the family could only pray would end by Christmas.

I feel like a fool, Hannah thought, honking the boat's electric horn for at least the fortieth time. Beaver Island had disappeared in the fog behind her, and Laketon had not yet appeared up ahead. But Hannah did not feel that she was boating blind, exactly. She could see the pewter gray water stretch for several boat lengths ahead, and the boat's compass told Hannah that she was headed in the right direction.

Hannah's mind ran over the many times she'd peered across the three miles of lake water to view the lights of Laketon before going to bed. The lights of Main Street marched up the hill from the municipal dock, and here and there a neon sign winked red and white, promoting business on the edge of the endless woods.

Laketon, even at a distance, seemed to Hannah an intrusion on the quiet life of Beaver Island. And with the attention Hannah had received since the sale of the Lee china, she felt almost as if someone were looking over her shoulder with every move.

For some moments Hannah enjoyed the solitude of this ride in the fog. The motor purred quietly enough so that the slush, slush, slush of the water on the hull settled her, calmed her.

The fog lifted a bit. Hannah opened the throttle just a little. This drifting in a gossamer cocoon was beginning to get tiresome.

The fog soon dropped again, but Hannah made no move to throttle back. The silly horn would scare everything for miles, anyway.

There it was! Hannah spun the wheel with all the strength of her good arm. Unable to brace herself with her other arm, which was in a sling, she lost her balance and nearly fell from her seat. The spray of a bright red paddle wheel trailing after a ghostly white steamboat left Hannah dripping wet.

Plainly, in gold letters along its side, was painted, *President Lincoln*. The steamboat let out a shrill blast from its whistle that almost made Hannah jump out of her skin. Then it vanished.

Hannah slapped her face like she'd seen Papa do to himself when he got sleepy driving to the antique auction in New York in Uncle Joe's car. But she was already wide awake! She shut the gas back and drifted, listening. But no noises came out of the fog.

"How's ze rib?" Uncle Joe asked, moments later, as Hannah pulled into the Laketon municipal dock. "Reckon Burt Buker'll think twice before he tangles with you agin, *non*?" he added without waiting for Hannah to answer. "Ol' Judge Blaisdell refused to let him post bond pending trial, so he's locked up," Uncle Joe added. "Said he's ze menace to society."

Hannah let this torrent of words soak in while she climbed into Uncle Joe's pickup truck. "Mama'd be hard put without you to help me with the grocery shopping this fall," Hannah said at last. "I'm kind o' helpless until this silly rib heals."

"Wa-al," Uncle Joe drawled, "you got y' Papa's motorboat across ze lake. That's got t' count for something, unless groceries can fly, *non*?"

"Uncle Joe?" Hannah inquired as they arrived at Northland Supermarket.

"Yes?"

Hannah let her thoughts run around in her head for a moment, enjoying the truck's heater after the boat ride in freezing weather. "Do...do people sometimes see things they think about a lot? Really, truly see them—even *feel* and hear them?" she rushed ahead.

"Well now...."

"Like the *President Lincoln*. I passed it so close in the mist that I got drenched by the spray from its paddle wheel." Hannah patted her wet sleeve as evidence. "And I *heard* its steam whistle."

Uncle Joe took a deep breath. "Let's go into ze store," he said.

"I know I *saw* a steamboat on the lake this morning," Hannah said as she and Uncle Joe drove back toward the dock with the groceries. Hannah interrupted Uncle Joe's talking because she was tired of his question about how things were going on Beaver Island.

"Well...it *warn't* the *President Lincoln.* That's still on ze bottom of ze lake, what they ain't carted off to St. Louis."

"But I *heard* a whistle. Didn't you hear a whistle?" Hannah insisted.

"Wa-al," Uncle Joe admitted, "I heard several boat horns while I was waitin' for you. Feller'd have t' be crazy *not* to blow his horn, boatin' in zat fog— thick as clam chowder, *non?*"

"This one sounded exactly like one of those steam whistles you have on that old recording of railroad sounds," Hannah protested. "Only much louder."

"Come to think of it, I *may* have heard zat, but zere are so many boat horns on zees lake I don't pay much attention. Zere's a feller that lives in a cottage way down—*miles* down ze lake—who has an air horn tuned to sound like a steam whistle. But he'd be crazy to travel this far in the fog, *non.*"

"Well, the fog's lifted now," Hannah brightened. "Mama'll be glad to see these groceries. I wish I could help you load them," she said sincerely.

"Oh, hey! Can't forget zees." Uncle Joe pulled a long, slender box from beneath his truck seat. "I told y' mom I'd let Walt hev it when he got big enough to be responsible. Eighty power. I got me a pair o' binoculars, so I don't need it no longer."

Big enough to be responsible. How Uncle Joe talks! Hannah thought as she purred across the now clear lake. Still, she realized that since he and Aunt Theresa had no kids, Mama's kids must seem to them to grow up pretty fast.

Hannah had a good idea what the box contained, so she merely passed it to Walt when she reached the dock.

"Can't open it now, sis. Got t' unload these groceries. Just leave it with my stuff in the back hall," said Walt, handing the box back.

Before supper, Hannah went to her bedroom to change into a clean dress. She would be a one-armed waitress, serving Mama's guests as best she could. On opening the door, she spotted something mounted on a tripod beside her window. "What's Walt been up to this time?" Hannah said aloud, indignant that her brother had entered her room without permission. Then she realized that it was the old telescope Uncle Joe had given Walt.

Might's well take a peek, Hannah thought. It occurred to her that her room had the best view of the lake in Beaver Lodge, so she understood why Walt had set up his telescope there.

Hannah adjusted the lens. Walt had left it pointed at a group of cottages several miles down the lake. Slowly she moved the telescope along the shoreline, marveling at how specks in the distance stood out. The specks became trees, boulders, cars, and cottages.

Then she saw it, profiled against a rocky cliff, riding at anchor. It was the *President Lincoln*—no doubt about it.

"Uncle Joe," Hannah cried into the phone, as soon as she got downstairs. "Quick! Before the sun goes down! Get your binoculars and go up to your attic window. Take a look at what's anchored next to a cliff, just below that green cottage with the brown roof maybe five miles down the lake," she squealed.

"This'll be the last trip with our boat until spring," said Papa. It was Thanksgiving Day, and the family was preparing to buzz across to the mainland to eat with Uncle Joe and Aunt Theresa. "If we hurry, we can see Laketon's Thanksgiving Day parade."

Laketon had just added a special parade as a local celebration, which even pulled folks away from the famous Macy's parade on TV to stand on the sidewalk in the cold. It was the Northwoods Sportsmen's Parade, and hunters who had just shot a deer or a moose would parade Main Street with the animal stretched across the hood of their car.

Several floats had been planned to liven up the show. No one knew what to expect, but Hannah's family had heard a rumor, which Uncle Joe refused to confirm or deny, that Joe Boudreau was driving his own float in the parade.

"Joe can't have much of a float," said Papa. "All he has to drive is that old pickup, and he's been so busy all fall working as a handyman that he'd hardly have time to build a float."

Uncle Joe and Aunt Theresa's car was in the driveway when the Parmenters arrived in Laketon. But the Boudreaus' garage stood open and Uncle Joe's old pickup was gone.

"Let's hurry," Aunt Theresa fretted. "We don't want to miss Joe's float."

Deer and moose aplenty were on display in the parade. A truck rolled by with two men dressed in red shirts as old-time lumberjacks. They pulled a long crosscut saw back and forth, cutting a log the old-fashioned way. Then came a model of the white church where the Parmenters and Boudreaus worshipped, mounted on a low trailer drawn by a garden tractor.

Where is Uncle Joe? Hannah wondered. Then she saw it.

The steamboat *President Lincoln*—only it was much smaller than the real *President Lincoln*—rolled past, slow, stately, handsome. Right in front of Hannah, the steamboat let out a blast that Aunt Theresa said later should have frightened every deer in the parade back to life. Hannah had heard that blast before!

"Hey!" yelled Walt, pointing to wheels with rusty hubcaps peeking out beneath the gliding replica of the *President Lincoln*. "Uncle Joe's truck!"

"You gave your old uncle a great idea, honey," Uncle Joe told Hannah over Thanksgiving dinner. "Once I saw zat steamboat in my binoculars, I knew what you'd seen on ze lake warn't no ghost. So I drove down zere ze next morning. Feller that built her was just packin' t' winter in Florida. He'd spent several weeks building this contraption out o' plywood an' bolting it onto an old cabin cruiser boat. So I made him an offer he couldn't refuse. An' ze paddle wheel, she really turns."

"How'd he know what the real *President Lincoln* looks like?" asked Hannah. "Diving when the salvage crew wasn't around, I suppose."

"Oh, no. Sence you've been showin' those china dolls—y' twelve apostles—over t' ze library, word's got out that old Miss Farnsworth has been hoarding a collection of stuff from Captain Pherson's estate. It includes a scrapbook with several good snapshots o' ze boat that now sits on ze bottom of ze lake. So he used ze photos."

"Oh," said Hannah, remembering Miss Farnsworth's locked box at the library.

"But however did you get your truck under it to drive it on the street?" Mama asked in surprise.

"It's just a big painted plywood box over a wooden frame, 'cept for the paddle wheel," Uncle Joe laughed. "She didn't take much changin' t' swap her from ze boat to fit my truck."

"What on earth are you going to do with your white elephant, Joe?" Papa laughed.

Hannah knew that whenever Papa used the term *white elephant*, he meant anything impractical, useless, and a nuisance to have around. She laughed out loud.

"Hey, I been considering it," Uncle Joe said with a chuckle. "Now that Laketon is getting a bit of publicity over ze *President Lincoln*, I might as well cash in on it, *non*? She would make a dandy excursion boat for paying passengers next summer, don't y' think, *non*?"

Uncle Joe seemed extremely pleased with his new toy, but Hannah was not impressed. A plywood box is a plywood box, she decided. The real *President Lincoln* lay at the bottom of Moosehead Lake. It was *her* steamboat, and nothing could ever change that, she told herself, not noticing that pride was beginning to replace the pleasure that once had been hers when she and Walt found the steamboat.

Chapter Fourteen

Hannah Is Famous

"Hold your head up. Say 'dolls.'"

Hannah grinned broadly and did as the news photographer had asked, as she lovingly held the Apostles Petie and Andrea in her lap. Old Miss Farnsworth sat in a chair next to Hannah and held the two china dolls that had stood in the glass cabinet at the Laketon public library for fifty years. The other ten dolls were carefully arranged on a table behind Hannah and the aged librarian.

The young woman from the *Bangor Daily News* popped her camera's flash in the faces of Hannah and Miss Farnsworth until they were both nearly blind. She lined up the fourteen dolls up and shot their portrait as a group, then one at a time.

"You've named your dolls after Christ's twelve apostles, I understand," said the reporter, scribbling in shorthand on her pad.

"I sure have," Hannah glowed. She passed the newswoman a slip of paper on which she'd jotted the names of her twelve.

"And these?" The reporter examined the library's two dolls in their antique, faded dresses.

"We just call them the Pherson dolls, dearie," Miss Farnsworth said. "Until Miss Parmenter here found the old captain's steamboat, hardly anybody hereabouts had even heard of Elihu Pherson."

"I call them Pauline and Barnie, after Paul and Barnabas," Hannah said, grinning.

"When will this story run in the paper, Miss?" asked Mama, who had come to Laketon with Hannah for the interview and photo session.

"Tomorrow, I expect," the woman replied. "I'm also going to send the story over the wire to the Associated Press. It could make national news."

"Not headlines, I hope," said Hannah, who had had quite enough publicity.

"Gracious, no," Mama agreed.

That evening at supper, Mama related to Papa what the reporter had said about the story running in the state's largest daily newspaper.

"And she's going to send it to the Associated Press," giggled Hannah. It was fun to think about being famous, even if having all those strange people fawning over you was a mite obnoxious, Hannah decided.

"Hmm-mmm!" Papa fretted. "The story will be statewide news tomorrow and national news the day after. Those dolls would be safer locked in a bank vault."

"O-o-o-o-o-o-o," empathized Hunter.

If Hunter feels Papa's worry that badly, maybe I should worry, too, Hannah thought.

And she did.

On cold January nights, Hunter often slept on the foot of Hannah's bed. Right after he'd had his weekly bath and flea treatment, he sometimes even dreamed his doggie dreams with his flop-eared head on Hannah's pillow.

But dog and mistress had nightmares together this night. Long after midnight, Hannah rose and crept to her window. The moon was full over the frozen lake, with a cottony cloud here and there to add extra beauty to God's good earth. Hannah squinted through Walt's telescope, pointing it across the lake at the clock tower on Laketon's old town hall. 'A quarter past two' she read clearly, though the clock was nearly four miles away.

Hannah next focused the telescope at the public library, across the street from the town hall. In the glow of the streetlight, the library's front door stood starkly out. My apostles—are they sleeping safely tonight? Hannah's heart mourned. Shortly before the lake froze for the winter, Hannah had lent them to the library for public display.

At last Hannah slipped back to her bedside. In the moonlight, she knelt to pray: "Dear Jesus, keep my twelve apostles safe. And whatever happens, I wish to honor You." Giving Hunter a heartfelt hug, Hannah fell fast asleep.

"Why not just trust the Lord to take care of them?" Hannah asked at breakfast the next morning. Papa had just stated that he or Mama should go to Laketon at once to bring the twelve apostles home. He feared theft. Besides, it was a new year, and the library had had them quite long enough, he concluded.

"We can't get them today. The library's not open," Mama protested. "It's open only three days a week."

"I'm sure the town clerk has a key," Papa said.

"She'll let me in—I pay them enough in taxes." Papa smiled wryly.

"But Papa, I *prayed* for my dolls last night."

"So did I," Papa affirmed. "And we *do* trust the Lord. But in a world of sinners, we keep our doors locked, we use secret bank account numbers...."

"And we bring our valuable dolls home, at least until the publicity blows over," Mama finished Papa's sentence.

"Except at Beaver Lodge, where we don't need to lock anything up," chuckled Walt.

Mama hugged her two children together. "That's one reason we brought you kids to live on Beaver Island. We wanted you to grow up in a world where you don't always have to look over your shoulder," she murmured.

That morning Hannah rode with Papa across the frozen lake on his snowmobile. Father and daughter went straight to the town office, where the clerk obligingly left her desk to cross the street and let them into the library. She waited until Papa and Hannah had taken Hannah's twelve apostles, then locked the door after them.

Once the dolls were safely in a locked chest on the sled behind his snowmobile, Papa stopped at the White Pine Pharmacy, where he bought two newspapers. There it was at the bottom of page one: "Beaver Island Girl Has Rare Doll Collection." The article went on to tell that the "twelve apostles" were in the Laketon public library "on temporary loan."

Papa next took Hannah to visit Miss Farnsworth. He showed her the article, giving her one of the newspapers.

"I suggest very strongly that you or the regular librarian place those two dolls in the bank vault at

Northland Trust Company, at least for a few months," Papa said.

Miss Farnsworth would hear none of it. "Our dolls have been quite comfortable in their glass case for fifty years. They'll be just fine there for another fifty," she tartly enunciated.

Next morning, Papa was not at all surprised to receive a phone call from the regular librarian. "You took *our* dolls, too," she snapped. "Miss Farnsworth said for you to leave them where they were."

Papa was not able to talk sense to the librarian, who refused to believe that the dolls' disappearance was the work of thieves. He phoned Sheriff Hobson at once. An hour later, the sheriff phoned back to say that the thief had broken a window in the storeroom to let himself into the library. He had also forced the lock of the dolls' glass case. And the town clerk told the sheriff that she had seen the dolls still in their case when she locked the door after Papa and Hannah left.

"I'm glad they didn't take Miss Farnsworth's box of Pherson stuff," Hannah said with relief, after she'd heard Papa's report.

The next morning, Mama beat Hannah to the phone. In the two days since the theft of the library's dolls, Hannah had taken a couple of phone calls in which the caller hung up without speaking.

"Somebody's trying to find out if we're home, no doubt," Papa concluded. "They want to steal our dolls, too." He made a point of insisting that Hannah keep the twelve apostles in a locked closet after that.

"No," Hannah heard Mama say firmly, "you may *not* have an interview for your magazine."

Hannah stood in front of Mama, making a time-out sign.

"Excuse me," Mama told the man on the phone. "Yes?" she said to Hannah.

"Can we *please* talk about it and call the man back?" Hannah begged.

"Don't call us. We'll call you if we change our minds," Mama said, returning to the long-distance phone conversation. "Sir," she added, "I have great respect for *The Saturday Evening Post*. You'll get the interview if anyone does." Then Mama hung up.

"The *Post*, Mama! They made Norman Rockwell famous for his *Post* covers, and he's my very favorite painter."

Hannah stared in tearful dismay at the painting that Mama kept above her kitchen range. It was of a boy thawing a frozen well pump with a teakettle. A tricolored hound, almost exactly like Hunter, shivered next to the well curb beside the boy. The painting was the whole family's favorite Rockwell. Hannah could easily imagine her twelve apostles on the cover of the Post.

"I'm sorry," Mama murmured.

Whatever Mama had intended to say next Hannah did not hear. "That's not *fair!*" Hannah screamed, stomping from the kitchen.

There! I said it! Hannah told herself as she trudged up the stairs to her room. Hannah believed that Mama considered "not fair" as bad as swearing—or worse.

Hannah lay on her bed crying for nearly an hour. Finally she got up, remembering Hunter on his chain out in the cold. She needed to let her hound in for a bowl of dog food and hot, leftover gravy.

Papa's voice rumbled from the kitchen as Hannah reached the lower hall. "We can't hide from crooks and news reporters forever," he said. "Perhaps we should just grant the interview, then take special care for a few months that we don't get robbed."

Mama, ever the worrywart, reminded Papa of the wilderness cottages just north of the lake that had been burglarized only last month, right after their owners returned to the city for the winter.

The conversation stopped when Hannah walked in. Papa sat silently sipping coffee.

"Sorry, Mama," said Hannah. "I was wrong to be rude." Hannah marched straight across the kitchen to the outside door to let Hunter in.

Mama hugged Hannah as soon as she returned. "We'll work something out," Mama said.

A week later, the sheriff phoned Papa to say that the crooks who stole the library's dolls had been caught in Boston. An antique dealer there recognized the dolls from the Associated Press article with the photo of Hannah, Miss Farnsworth, and the fourteen china dolls. The dealer reported the men who had tried to sell him the dolls to the FBI. The police soon discovered that they had broken a major ring of antique thieves. To the Parmenters' relief, the crank phone calls stopped coming at once.

"I think," said Papa carefully at supper that evening, "the time has come when we may consider granting an interview to the *Post.*"

"I'll phone their editor in the morning," Mama agreed.

Hannah was a bit disappointed when the reporter identified himself as a writer from the *Maine Sunday Telegram,* in Portland. "I thought they'd send a writer from Indianapolis," said Hannah.

"I *do* write for *The Saturday Evening Post*," explained the smiling young man with the camera and notepad. The reporter produced two business cards: one said *Telegram*, and the other said *Post*. Both cards had his name on them. "I'm what they call a stringer," he explained. "*The Saturday Evening Post's* editor phones me whenever he needs a special story done north of Boston. This is the first time I've had to drive a snowmobile across a lake to get an interview," he added, laughing.

❋ ❋ ❋ ❋ ❋ ❋ ❋

"People, you won't believe this!" Walt had just returned from Laketon on the snowmobile with several bags of feed for Molly, her calves, and the chickens. "Look here!" He unrolled a copy of the *Maine Sunday Telegram* that the reporter had mailed to the Parmenters' post office box in Laketon.

"MOOSEHEAD LAKE GIRL RESTORES RARE DOLLS" read the headline for the bottom half of the front page. "Hannah Parmenter, of Beaver Island near Laketon, has found what is perhaps the rarest collection of antique china dolls anywhere in America," the story read. "Diving in Moosehead Lake with her brother Walter, Hannah last summer found the legendary lost steamboat, the *President Lincoln*. Sister and brother returned to the shipwreck site in late fall for a cold-water dive. Hannah herself discovered the treasure chest containing Capt. Elihu Pherson's precious dolls, missing for more than half a century," the article went on.

"Hannah, you're famous!" laughed Walt, slapping his sister on the back.

"Ouch!" was all she could reply through tears of joy. Just then Hannah was busy opening the other large package Walt had found in their P.O. box. It was a proof copy of a two-page article to appear in *The Saturday Evening Post* with color photos of Hannah and her dolls. A letter to Hannah from the editor said that the piece would "run in the Spring issue, available on newsstands everywhere in March."

Chapter Fifteen

Raise the Titanic

"Raise the *Titanic!*"

"Look at this, Mama." Hannah laid an article from *Seafarer's Magazine* on the kitchen table one day late in January. The article had arrived in a letter from Mr. Parrish in St. Louis. And right at the beginning of the story was a photo of the Shipwreck Man, the professor whom Hannah and Mama had met at the Maine state library in Augusta.

Mama looked over her daughter's shoulder as Hannah read aloud the interview with the professor, famous discoverer of the *Titanic* and the *Luisitania.*

"When that great ship struck an iceberg and sank in 1912, it became forever the sacred tomb of some 1,500 people who lost their precious lives," the Shipwreck Man told a reporter from *Seafarer's Magazine* in an interview. "Instead, we should film the wreck of the *Titanic* with underwater TV cameras so that the whole world may view the tragedy of this majestic ship," the professor said. "We can study the *Titanic* for science and history, yet still leave the watery grave of these poor people undisturbed," he argued.

The article went on to say that some shipwreck salvage experts had devised a way that the *Titanic* might be raised from beneath a mile of seawater by using inflatable pontoons. But the professor, who had helped develop underwater TV exploration as a science, strongly protested this idea.

"And just look at that!" cried Hannah.

The article showed an old photo of the *Titanic* as a brand-new ship. Next to that picture another photo showed the ship broken in half on the ocean bottom.

"My *President Lincoln* broke in half when it sank, just like the *Titanic*," Hannah said, surprised.

Next she read Mr. Parrish's letter. "Oh, my!" Hannah exclaimed about halfway through the first page. "He and Mr. Duke want to come back to Maine to raise the *President Lincoln*."

"I wouldn't think there'd be anything left to raise, after all the stuff the salvage crew has taken," Mama commented. "And that underwater explosion—where Burt Buker and that Lem fellow used dynamite? Didn't it destroy a lot of the boat?"

"No-oh!" Hannah knew for sure that Buker, for all his dastardly deed, had done little damage to the *President Lincoln*. "He just blew a few loose boards around. The Maine State Police divers said that Buker is such an amateur that most of his fuses got wet, so very little of the dynamite went off."

"And you know what?" Hannah went on.

"What?"

"After the salvagers got the heavy steam engines lifted out, plus a lot of other stuff—winches, chains, brass hardware—the steamboat is actually much lighter. It'll be easier to raise now."

"I don't know," said Mama. "Raising an old steamboat after all those years on the bottom of the lake. They plan to start in the spring, I suppose."

"Next week!" Hannah's eyes positively glowed with delight as she spoke. "And I guess now that I've rescued the twelve drowned apostles, even the professor couldn't object to raising the *President Lincoln*," Hannah laughed.

※ ※ ※ ※ ※ ※ ※

"Walt, you'll need to bring your ice-fishing auger to bore holes," Hannah said. "I'll get a yardstick to measure the thickness of the ice and a shovel to clear the snow."

"Don't forget a compass. I still remember how frightened Mama and Papa were when you got lost in the blowing snow out by my fishing shanty. They were about to call out a search party."

Walt straightened up from pouring gasoline into Papa's snowmobile. He and Hannah peered across Moosehead's vast expanse of snow-blanketed ice stretching to the horizon. Here and there chilly whirlwinds were swishing up loose snow, blowing it madly around. The sun shone brightly this marvelous winter day on Beaver Island. But people down on the lake ice fishing often found themselves blinded for some moments by these small blizzards.

"Y' say your men from Missouri now wish to

raise the hulk of the *President Lincoln*—in midwinter, yet?" Papa shook his head in astonishment.

"Sure do, Papa," said Hannah, who had come into the house to get a compass. "That's why they're asking me and Walt to measure the ice to see if it's thick enough to drive a truck on safely. They believe it'll be much easier than using pontoons during warm weather, like the people who wish to raise the *Titanic* want to do."

"Well, I guess it does make sense," Papa said slowly. "I seem to remember reading that the Russians put a whole convoy of trucks on the ice to supply the city of Leningrad with food during World War II."

"It *will* work, Papa." Hannah kissed her father's bristly cheek. "They plan to drag the *President Lincoln* to shore after it's dried in the sun for a few weeks."

"I still find it odd that it's *Southerners* raising a steamboat from a frozen lake," Papa chuckled.

※ ※ ※ ※ ※ ※ ※

The activity on Moosehead Lake brought TV camera crews, newspaper photographers, and magazine writers from all over New England and even from New York. Since the men from Missouri had to hire a snowplow to make a road across the five miles of ice to get their rented crane out there, the reporters also had a road to use. Instead of renting snowmobiles in Laketon, the newsmen simply barreled across the ice in their cars.

The work went on all day and all night for two days. Mr. Parrish and Mr. Duke knew that once the hole was cut in the ice, they had to work around the clock before it froze up again.

Hannah sat by her bedroom window late the second night watching the progress. Though it was after midnight, cars could still be seen traveling back and forth from Laketon to the shipwreck site. "Interstate 95," Papa sarcastically called this road on the ice.

Hannah pointed Walt's telescope at the work. Several frogmen in wet suits were illuminated in the powerful floodlights that lit the ice like a football field. These men in winter scuba outfits appeared to be getting ready to dive and attach cables from the crane to the *President Lincoln*, it seemed to Hannah.

"Hannah, wake up!" Mama was shaking her awake. Hannah squinted at the luminous digital dial on her bedside clock radio. "3:45."

"Is the house on fire?"

"No," laughed Mama. "The *President Lincoln* is coming up in just a few minutes."

"So?" Hannah groaned. "I'll look at it in the morning." Before she had gone to bed, Hannah would have given almost anything to be present when her steamboat rose from its watery berth. But sleepy folks don't always make sense.

"Hannah!" Mama spoke firmly but kindly now. "They want you there with one of your dolls."

"Who...who on earth wants me?"

"The TV camera crews. They want you on the morning news. *Good Morning America* and *Today* are both there! Papa's getting the snowmobile ready right now. Mr. Duke just called here on his mobile phone."

At a quarter to seven that morning, Hannah and

Walt were pounding on Uncle Joe and Aunt Theresa's door in Laketon. Hannah hadn't slept a wink since she'd stood shivering in the floodlights while first the rear section of the *President Lincoln* and then the paddle wheels rose on cables behind her. Brother and sister would now watch Hannah and the steamboat on *Good Morning America*, if they could just wake Uncle Joe up to let them use his TV set.

Chapter Sixteen

Cap'n Joe's "Attraction"

Hannah, Walt, Mama, and Papa were taking turns using Walt's telescope two days after the rear section of the steamboat was raised. Two of Mama's hotel guests who had binoculars had joined the Parmenter family in Hannah's room to watch the workers pull up the front section. It was late afternoon, and the vessel was silhouetted in the setting sun as, dripping with water and weeds, the handsome relic arose from its grave.

"What are they doing, Papa?" Walt had not seen the other half raised. He was surprised to see men with hoses rushing around to squirt the ship as if it were on fire.

"Washing sixty years of sediment off before it freezes," Papa explained. "Hannah and I watched them do this the other night, but the TV stations didn't show it."

The spectators held their breath. The front section teetered and shook as powerful tractors moved it away from the hole in the ice. Then the crew

106

rushed over to the tail section, preparing to push the two halves together so that the *President Lincoln* would look like a complete steamboat once again.

Mr. Parrish had already told Hannah that he planned to leave the steamer on the ice to dry as much as possible, then return from Missouri to move it to shore before the spring rains came. He had purchased an old empty warehouse to store the ship in after it was dried out. Mr. Parrish, Mr. Duke, Hannah, and Walt would jointly donate the *President Lincoln* to the Town of Laketon. School-children from all over Maine would be able to see what a genuine riverboat looked like in the days when Mark Twain wrote *Life on the Mississippi.*

"It's *huge*," Hannah marveled when she saw the *President Lincoln* on the ice the next morning, its two halves pushed together to make one ship. When she and Walt arrived, Mr. Parrish and Mr. Duke were already there directing the salvage crew in shoring up the bulky steamboat, using dozens of used telephone poles and hundreds of old tires to keep it sitting upright.

"Look at the size of that paddle wheel!" It was Papa speaking to Mama. They had just arrived on a second snowmobile, which Papa had bought to meet the needs of his growing business at Beaver Lodge.

"And the wheel *still* has some of its original red paint after all these years," Mama marveled.

"That's where I dropped my flashlight," Hannah pointed out. "The *President Lincoln* was lying on her side underwater. The space between the wheel and the ship's stern looked like a deep cave."

Saturday morning Hannah went to her room to change into clean clothes after her turn milking

Molly in the barn. She peered out over the lake at the wreck of the *President Lincoln.*

Then she saw it.

Not again! thought Hannah in disgust.

But there it was, black smoke rolling from twin stacks, the steam whistle tooting away. It was the plywood replica of the *President Lincoln.* First it floats. Then it goes up Main Street. Now it travels across the ice. Will it fly next? Hannah wondered angrily. "My steamboat is the real *President Lincoln,*" she told herself half aloud.

The plywood *President Lincoln II* stopped in front of the real *President Lincoln.* Hannah quickly grabbed Walt's telescope and focused it for a close-up look. A door opened in the side, and a dozen people piled out into the snow. Last of all came a man in a Navy pea coat and a captain's cap.

Though Hannah watched the man closely, she could not quite make out his features. He had a thin, grey beard, however. And he walked with a limp. She had seen enough. It was Uncle Joe Boudreau starting his lake excursion season a few months early!

Hannah hurried downstairs to tell Mama. She found her in the kitchen with Papa, who had just returned from an early morning trip to Laketon for supplies. The *Laketon Weekly Gazette* was spread out on the kitchen table.

"See here, Hannah," said Papa before she could blurt out what she'd seen out on the lake. Papa held up the newspaper.

There on the front page was a boxed ad. It was a photo of the phony *President Lincoln* with a smaller photo of Uncle Joe set into it. "See the Greatest Attraction North of Boston, Hosted by Cap'n Joe," the ad said. "$10 for a 2-hour Ride-Tour of the Only Steamboat Ever to Set on Ice." Then followed one of Uncle Joe's silly jokes:

"The *Titanic*—Ice Took Her Down.

The *President Lincoln*—Ice Holds Her Up."

"Your brother-in-law has quite a sense of humor," Papa said to Mama.

"He's being ridiculous," Hannah snorted.

Then they all had a good laugh.

"Uncle Joe might as well have his fun," Hannah sighed. "But it does get pretty tiresome, all those people driving out there just to gawk."

Hannah worried, though, that somehow Uncle Joe's plywood steamboat would steal attention from her real *President Lincoln*. I have a *right* to be proud of my steamboat, she told herself.

"The traffic does get tiresome," agreed Mama. "But his 'official' excursions may help keep vandalism down."

✳ ✳ ✳ ✳ ✳ ✳ ✳

"Best piece o' corned beef I've ever sunk my teeth into," praised Uncle Joe on Sunday afternoon. On Sundays when there were no guests to feed at Beaver Lodge, Hannah and her family would often eat Sunday dinner with the Boudreaus in Laketon. Today Aunt Theresa fixed the all-time favorite winter meal of both families: New England-style boiled dinner. She started with a five-pound chunk of corned beef brisket, which simmered on the stove all night. Next morning she added vegetables. There were potatoes, carrots, turnips, onions—and of course lots of cabbage.

Aunt Theresa had just left the table to cut the

raspberry pie, a hearty ten-incher made from berries frozen fresh from her summer garden patch. "Yes sir," Uncle Joe rambled on. "Makes a man feel his youth again, *non?*"

Hannah giggled. Does the corned beef Uncle Joe ate *before* he got his false teeth also count? she wondered. She knew that her uncle had had his dentures only a few months.

"I have to get a closer look at your version of the *President Lincoln*," said Papa, who had suddenly become genuinely interested in Uncle Joe's attraction. "Where are you keeping it?"

"Oh, it's in ze old Hardin Company warehouse, up back o' ze village."

"Isn't that the warehouse we...I mean Mr. Parrish and Mr. Duke have purchased—where they plan to display the *President Lincoln* in the spring?" Hannah asked. She'd been in the warehouse with her friends from St. Louis. But Hardin Company meant nothing to her.

"Shore is." Uncle Joe eyed Hannah with concern. "Hardin built it in 1937. It's been empty since '72. Ze sign she's gone, but everybody still calls it that. Guess you didn't know that. Mr. Parrish, he gave me permission to use it until spring," he added quickly.

"I didn't know that either," Hannah said quietly. She and Mr. Parrish had taken the brass sign that Hannah and Walt had found on the *President Lincoln* to a sign painter. They planned to have a large copy of the original sign with its raised letters made to go above the warehouse door. It would say "President Lincoln" in letters large enough to be read from blocks away. Hardin Company indeed! Hannah thought, sulking silently, her pride wounded.

After the last piece of raspberry pie had been eaten, the whole family piled into Aunt Theresa's Buick for the ride to the warehouse. Uncle Joe put on his sailor's cap and drove. "I'm Cap'n Joe now," he chuckled.

"Take a peek inside her," Uncle Joe said happily. He opened a door in the side from which Hannah had seen passengers scramble on Saturday.

Hannah let Walt and Papa follow Uncle Joe through the door, then slipped in after them. Mama and Aunt Theresa, however, stayed outside this boat on wheels, enjoying the view of the carefully painted false railings and portholes that had looked real enough to Hannah that morning in the fog.

Hannah was surprised when she saw Uncle Joe's truck. Or at least it *had* once been a truck. Uncle Joe had built a platform on which he'd bolted a dozen padded seats. The passengers could peer out through holes in the plywood steamboat that from the outside appeared to be real steamboat windows.

Uncle Joe climbed a ladder to a wheelhouse on top of the structure. Using cables, belts, and pulleys, he had rigged his old truck to be driven slowly from up there. He steered with a real ship's wheel.

"I can unfasten this here plywood *President Lincoln II* and easily bolt her right onto my boat fer lake excursions all next summer," Cap'n Joe chuckled.

"Wow!" said Walt. "Cool!"

"Huh" was Hannah's response to her brother's enthusiasm. *Silly*, she was thinking.

"Sounds like a winner. Looks like you've got it both ways," said Papa, talking to Uncle Joe, who had stuck his head out of the wheelhouse window.

"Hey, Uncle Joe, how do you get smoke to come from your stacks, since you don't have a steam engine?" Walt's mechanical mind was curious. Hannah hadn't thought about it. Aren't smoke-stacks *supposed* to belch smoke? she wondered.

"Them's really stovepipes painted black," Uncle Joe answered modestly. "I hooked ze truck's exhaust pipe into zem. When I want smoke, I just open a special valve to pour dirty old engine oil into ze exhaust. Makes her smoke big-time," Uncle Joe said enthusiastically.

"That's pollution," Hannah said flatly.

"Hey, can we get ze warehouse door open? Let's take her for a ride, *non*?" Cap'n Joe yelled from the wheelhouse, appearing not to have heard Hannah's remark.

Walt jumped out and ran for the switch to open the electric overhead door. Hannah climbed from the plywood steamboat after him. Mama and Aunt Theresa stepped in.

"Aren't you coming?" Aunt Theresa said before closing the door.

"Naw. I'm going for a walk. See you at the house." Hannah was glad that Mama had gone in ahead of her aunt. Mama would have insisted that Hannah come along.

Uncle Joe backed his contraption out of the warehouse, then waited while Walt closed the electric door and climbed aboard.

Hannah stayed inside the warehouse until Uncle Joe's plywood version of the *President Lincoln* disappeared down the road, belching black smoke as it rumbled along.

Hannah shuffled along unhappily at first, but

she soon realized that the trip that had taken just a few minutes in the Buick was really quite a long hike on a cold day. She hurried, jogging part of the way. Twice she skidded on the icy sidewalk and nearly fell.

The road led onto Main Street, and the Boudreau home was clear on the other side of the village by the waterfront. Halfway through town, Hannah found herself in front of the White Pine Pharmacy, where Papa sometimes bought newspapers and magazines.

The store was closed, but Hannah pressed her face against the glass door. By squinting, she could see the magazine rack. There was *The Saturday Evening Post*. Nope, Hannah thought. Same one as last week. When will the spring issue be out? she silently mourned. Just then in the glass Hannah caught the reflection of Aunt Theresa's Buick gliding past with Hannah's family riding in warm comfort.

Hannah was cold and miserable. Somehow, she wanted to be miserable.

Wounded pride doesn't get much sympathy, Hannah realized. But is it wrong for me to be proud of *my President Lincoln*? she pondered. Hannah could not at the time find an answer.

Chapter Seventeen

Fire on the Ice!

Hannah shivered in her flannel pajamas late that night as she peered at the snow-covered lake, but not from the cold. She watched the winking taillights of a pair of racing snowmobiles as they sailed past a lighted cottage across the lake, then shot past another farther down only seconds later.

A thrill ran up Hannah's spine as she considered that some of these light machines were tearing along at perhaps eighty miles an hour. A chill of fear mingled with this thrill when she remembered how, only last winter, two teens whom Walt had known were killed while ice racing out there where no drivers' licenses were needed and no speed limits were enforced.

Hannah crouched on the soft chair by her window and parted the curtains for another look. Not only was her bedroom much warmer in winter since Papa had installed the thermal-pane glass, but she could now peer through the frostless window far out across vast Moosehead Lake, even when the thermometer plunged way below zero.

The distant, wild roar of racing snowmobiles on the frozen lake had troubled her dreams this late Saturday night. It was after one in the morning, and tomorrow Hannah's family would themselves travel down the lake on Papa's snowmobile to worship at the Laketon Community Church. Now the red taillights of the speeding machines grew smaller and smaller in the distance, and at last they faded from view beyond Mt. Kineo.

The moon was full, and Hannah could see the wreck of the ruined *President Lincoln* starkly outlined against the lake's white blanket of snow. Monday, Hannah knew, was to be a special day. The old steamboat, raised from the lake bottom in two pieces, would be skidded behind several powerful tractors into Laketon's frozen port for the first time in nearly sixty years. Hannah planned to watch lovingly as her ship creaked along every foot of its icy way!

In the clear night, Hannah noticed a lone snowmobile approaching from near a string of closed-up summer cottages on a dead-end dirt road north of the lake. The snowmobile pulled behind the *President Lincoln*, where it stopped out of sight. This did not surprise Hannah. By now she was used to the curious sightseers, some of them on the ice late at night, who often came to gawk, and sometimes to steal a souvenir.

Hannah sighed aloud. On Monday, Mr. Duke and Mr. Parrish would arrive from St. Louis, where they were restoring the *General Grant*. They planned to push snow into Laketon's Main Street to make it slippery, working at night when there wouldn't be any traffic. Then with tractors and steel cables they would haul the boat's two halves up to the old warehouse. There a crew of men would bolt the halves of the old steamboat together as a tourist attraction. With the ship on display indoors, vandals would no longer be able to rob the *President Lincoln* of its precious treasures, Hannah was glad to know.

In the moonlight, Hannah could see a thin wisp of smoke rising from behind the old riverboat. She was not alarmed at first. Probably whoever it was was having trouble starting his overheated snowmobile, and the motor was smoking. But then she saw the snowmobile putter away from the ship where it lay on the ice, braced up with old telephone poles and worn-out auto tires. Hannah watched the snowmobile for a moment. The operator turned his machine around and stopped, as if to take a last look.

What's he up to? Hannah wondered.

She glanced again at the President Lincoln. The wisp of smoke had turned into a column. At its base, something glowed red!

Hannah raced for the stairs and slid down the banister, not waiting to wake her parents as she ran for the new cellular phone to dial emergency 911.

"I say let 'er burn," growled the Laketon fire chief. Chief Sylvester was speaking to one of his firefighters who was busily chopping a hole in the ice so that their pump truck could send a stream of water onto the burning wreck of the *President Lincoln*." She's ruined now," the chief said angrily. "Whatever doesn't burn will have to be cleaned up on dangerously thin ice."

"Mr. Sylvester," Hannah cried in dismay, "there must be something the fire department can do."

Chief Sylvester turned to Hannah, who had just hopped off Papa's snowmobile after riding across the lake with Walt.

"Honey," he said to the tearful girl, "this town owes you a lot for helping find a lost treasure. But I'm afraid all we've got to show for it now is some pictures." He pointed at the blazing *President Lincoln.* "Most of the smoke is from burning tires and timbers, which those fellers from St. Louis used to brace up your ship. No lives are in danger, so I'm not sending men in there to disappear into that smoke and put theirs in danger."

Hannah, through her tears, tried to understand, but she could not answer the chief.

"Let's go, Walt," she said sadly. "Mama and Papa will worry about us."

Walt swung the snowmobile around, and brother and sister raced toward the glow of Beaver Lodge's lighted windows.

Sunday came, and Hannah's family went to church. Hannah did not hear the sermon. What she did hear, over and over, was her heart telling her that she'd failed. The *President Lincoln* was to be Hannah's gift to her townsfolk. She had found the china, which was sold to keep Papa from losing Beaver Lodge to the bankers. And she had a dozen antique china dolls, the best collection anywhere, she had heard.

But Hannah was angry and bitter. If only Walt and I had thought to take turns tenting on the ice with the cellular phone to call for help if needed. If only I'd realized the crook was about to set my steamboat on fire.

If only. If only. If only. Mama had told Hannah before that "if onlies" are just Satan's way of keeping God's children looking backward, like Lot's wife, who turned to a pillar of salt while watching her city burn. Right now, though, Hannah did not care. She wanted to catch that crook and throw him in jail.

Chapter Eighteen

Hunter Bites
an Old Enemy

Hannah scurried around Monday morning to help Mama feed breakfast to the several winter vacationers at Beaver Lodge. Papa had given Hannah permission to take the snowmobile out to look over the ashes and debris where the President Lincoln had burned. Hannah had to agree to take Walt along—hardly necessary, since he was anxious to go, too.

"You'll have to wait here, boy," Hannah told Hunter. She pushed her hound inside as she and Walt left. Hunter had been out for a run after being cooped up in the house all night. The thermometer had fallen to twenty below zero Fahrenheit, and on these frost-bound winter nights Hunter's home under the porch, even with straw and old blankets, would not keep him warm.

"O-o-o-ooo," Hunter complained. Sadly he rolled his languid brown eyes up at Hannah and slunk inside.

"My turn to drive, big brother," Hannah stated

119

firmly, as she hopped into the snowmobile's driver's seat ahead of Walt. Walt had driven the night of the fire, after Papa had insisted that Hannah could not go without Walt. Hannah grudgingly admitted to herself that had Walt not driven she might have raced up too close to the flames and gotten hurt.

No new snow had fallen for more than a week, and the sky over Maine's northern woodland was cloudless and deep blue as Hannah pointed the snowmobile toward the frozen lake. A light westerly breeze numbed her cheeks, so that she hunkered down behind the windshield, thankful for her goose down-filled parka. She carefully eased the machine down the steep drive toward the ice-bound shore, as Papa had taught her. Hannah was about to open the throttle to race across the flat expanse of snow-covered ice when, "Whoa!" Walt yelled.

"What's up?" Hannah hit the brakes and cut the gas. She need not have asked. Hunter, squirming and shivering, hopped aboard and wriggled between Hannah and Walt.

"How'd you get loose, you rascal?" Hannah cried.

"One of the guests let him out, I'm sure," Walt said in disgust.

"Arf!" Hunter agreed, but not in disgust.

"Well, we're not takin' y' back!" With that, Hannah opened the gas, and Papa's snowmobile fairly flew toward the wreckage.

Hannah and Walt were not surprised to find Mr. Duke and Mr. Parrish there ahead of them. The men had arrived by plane from St. Louis on Sunday, and they had rented a snowmobile near where they stayed in Laketon. Though the men sometimes stayed at Beaver Lodge, they preferred

Laketon, since they needed to talk daily with their businesses in the big city.

"See here," said Mr. Parrish. He held up a metal five-gallon can. He smiled grimly. "Something the sheriff missed." He pointed toward the shore of the lake, a quarter of a mile away. "Found it behind a big rock, where it must've bounced off a snowmobile when the arsonist climbed the bank from the lake."

"Gas can?" Walt remarked. Lots of snowmobilers carry extra gas for wilderness trips, Walt knew.

"Nossuh. Y'all hev a whiff," Mr. Parrish drawled. He unscrewed the cap and held it up.

Hannah sniffed. "Kerosene. I've filled lamps with it for Mama many times."

"Right," Mr. Duke put in. "Best stuff there is to start a hot fire with. Arson—no doubt about it."

"Does the sheriff know?" Hannah asked.

"He suspects it, of course. We're taking this can to him for fingerprints."

"The crook had a snowmobile. I *saw* him," Hannah insisted.

"That's for sure," agreed Walt.

"Hun-ter-r-rr!" yelled Hannah, whistling. He was heading toward the nearest shore, his sharp snout pointing to the tracks of a snowshoe hare that had hopped past hours ago in the night.

Hunter stopped, raised his head obediently, then came bounding back.

"What about where you found the can? Wasn't there a snowmobile track?" Hannah asked.

"There was. Well preserved, too, since there hasn't been a flake of new snow, and this cold has prevented anything from melting," said Mr. Parrish.

"Can you show us?" Hannah asked. She surprised herself. She, not Walt, was asking most of the questions. If Nancy Drew can do it, I can do it, she thought confidently, remembering the famous girl detective books.

"Sure. Y'all wait, and I'll wind up Old Yeller, here."

Mr. Parrish jerked his thumb toward a garish yellow snowmobile with "Laketon Village Rentals" painted in black letters on the side.

"We were careful not to drive on the arsonist's track," Mr. Duke explained, after he and Mr. Parrish had taken Hannah, Walt, and Hunter around the ashes, away from Beaver Island. "All the other snowmobile tracks eventually lead back toward Laketon," he explained. "Except this one." He pointed toward a track, separate from the others, leading toward the boarded-up summer cottages on the dead-end road.

"You're right," Walt agreed.

"Arf!" observed Hunter.

"We followed the track about a mile back into the woods on the dirt road. There it joins tracks made by winter sportsmen. It's impossible to tell which snowmobile went where, after that."

"What *are* you doing?" Walt looked with surprise at Hannah, who was crawling on hands and knees in the snow.

"Look here!" Hannah cried.

The men and Walt stepped over to peer at Hannah's discovery.

"That snowmobile has a missing cleat in its track." Hannah pointed toward a gap in the track. A few feet farther on was another, then another, and another. The gaps were spaced evenly, and they continued on.

"Maybe you've got something," Walt agreed.

"This way we may be able to tell the crook's track from the other tracks."

"Walt, we've *got* to check it out," Hannah pleaded. She knew that Papa would never permit her to travel into the deep woods without Walt. In fact, Hannah was unsure if either of her parents would permit even Walt to go into the forest to track a crook.

"Awright," Walt agreed, hesitating. Even though he had helped discover the *President Lincoln* he was not nearly as angry as Hannah was when it burned.

"O-o-o-o-o-oo," whined Hunter, sensing Walt's discomfort.

"Wa-al," drawled Mr. Parrish, seeing that Hannah was anxious to do some detective work on her own, "we have got t' be getting to our motel. Y' all take care, an' don't mess with any crooks. See y'." He picked up the kerosene can, and the men roared off on their rented snowmobile.

Hannah again took the controls, and she followed the crook's snowmobile track up the lake bank and past the cottages. The track went into the woods exactly where she had seen the snowmobile go just as the fire started.

As the men from Missouri had said, about a mile back, where the cottage road joins a logging company truck road, the crook's snowmobile track became hopelessly tangled with many others.

"Uh, oh!" Hannah declared.

"Can't we follow any farther?" Walt asked.

"That's not the problem. Look at the gas gauge."

Hannah was upset with herself for being in such a hurry that she forgot to fill the tank.

"We'll be lucky to get back to Beaver Lodge," Walt agreed. Hannah checked her watch. "It's only ten o'clock. Mama and Papa won't worry, long's we're home by noon."

"You're crazy. We're about out of gas!"

"I don't mean drive, silly," Hannah answered hotly. Her *President Lincoln* had just burned. Like Nancy Drew, Hannah was going to get her man. "We can't look for the snowmobile track with the broken cleat while we're roaring along, anyway. We can walk for a mile or so. Maybe we'll find where Mr. Broken Cleat splits off from the others."

"If you say so," Walt said without enthusiasm. Part of him wanted to carry on. Another part wanted to go home. But Hannah's persistence told him he'd have a quarrel if they turned back now.

Half an hour's walk brought sister, brother, and hound to a fork in the road. Here, sure enough, the track with the broken cleat left the others. Just over a low rise was an abandoned logging camp, with several ramshackle buildings, most with roofs caved in.

Walt pointed silently to a low building apart from the others. Smoke curled from a stovepipe sticking through the roof. "Stay here," he ordered, suddenly protective of his little sister. "Hide under that big ol' hemlock. An' keep Hunter quiet." Walt pointed toward a snow-laden evergreen, its branches nearly to the ground. "I'm going to circle around for a better look," Walt whispered. "Snowmobile," his lips formed silently as he nodded toward where a yellow rented machine stood partly hidden next to the building.

Badly as she wanted to go with Walt, something deep within Hannah seemed to speak to her heart, warning her to wait. Hannah dragged Hunter under the overspreading hemlock, muzzling with her mittened hands his whimpers at the snow that poured off the branches onto his back. Walt had vanished into the underbrush by the time she got her hound settled.

Presently, Walt appeared, walking out of sight of the building's single window. He slipped up to the machine, raised the cover of the motor, and bent over it. Hannah could see that Walt was yanking at something with his hands, and she held her breath.

Suddenly, "Boinng!" The lid fell with a clatter as Walt straightened up.

The door of the shack flew open, and a shirtless man in long johns rushed barefoot outside carrying a rifle.

"Sic 'im, Hunter!" screamed Hannah, giving her hound a shove.

"Arf, arf, arf...R-R-R-R-R-RR!" Hunter leaped onto the man as he bolted around the corner of his shack. Hunter clawed, snapped, and snarled so that the crook must have thought he was being attacked by a rabid timber wolf.

The gun went off. Hunter rolled, then stumbled toward Hannah, still alive but bleeding.

Walt, who had ducked into the woods, suddenly returned. Racing up behind the startled man, he tore the gun from the man's hands just as the man raised it to fire at Hannah. Walt yanked the weapon open to unload it as he ran, then threw it into deep snow.

Cursing, the man dived into the cold snowbank after his now useless rifle.

"Guess you've tasted that nasty ol' man's blood before, haven't y' boy," Hannah said as soon as they realized they were not being followed.

"He has? When?" asked Walt, who in the excitement hadn't gotten a look at the fellow's face. Walt examined Hunter's wound, finding only a graze mark on the hound's back. "Here, I'll carry him for a while. Hunter saved my life."

"Yup. I saw the guy's face," Hannah panted. "It's Burt Buker, the fellow who went to prison for trying to kill me last fall. I thought they kept guys like him locked up in jail!" Hannah shuddered. Only now did it fully dawn on her what Buker might have done had Walt not grabbed the gun.

"That's not all," Walt said. "That snowmobile was stolen from Laketon Village Rentals—same place I rented that scuba outfit last summer. They don't rent them out overnight. I unhooked the spark plug wires, so he can't chase us with it."

Hunter was trotting with Hannah by the time the trio returned to Papa's snowmobile. Walt ran ahead and leaped into the seat. "C'mon," he yelled, as much to the machine that seemed slow to start in the bitter cold as to Hannah to hurry up. "We've got t' get to Laketon and notify the sheriff!"

Sheriff Bill Hobson already had the crook's kerosene can when Hannah and Walt arrived roaring down Main Street and skidding to a stop in front of the town hall just as Papa's snowmobile ran out of gas.

Without waiting for Hannah and Walt to fully explain themselves, the sheriff interrupted their story. "Buker broke out of prison sometime Friday night. We figger he stole a snowmobile from Village Rentals. Probably in Canada by now—there's a hundred places he could slip across the border through the woods. The Royal Canadian Mounted Police will pick him up, for sure." The sheriff leaned back in his swivel chair, confident of his analysis. "As you say, I'm sure he burned your steamboat.

But 'the Mounties always get their man,' as the old saying goes."

"Mr. Hobson," Hannah protested, angry now, "Burt Buker shot my hound, and he tried to shoot me! We've already found our man!"

"I fixed his stolen snowmobile so it won't run," Walt put in excitedly.

"Whoa! Where's he hiding out?"

Sheriff Hobson jumped from his chair and grabbed his radio to call his deputy.

Chapter Nineteen

A St. Valentine's Tragedy

"What will you do now?"

Hannah sat on the seat of Papa's snowmobile watching Mr. Duke and Mr. Parrish work with axes and heavy ice chisels. Many of the antique, hand-forged bolts that had held the *President Lincoln* together, had sunk, red hot, into the ice when the old steamboat burned. The men needed to chip some of these bolts free to use in restoring their other boat, the *General Grant.*

"Head back to St. Louis to work on the *General Grant,* I guess," Mr. Parrish chuckled.

"Once we get done collecting junk," laughed Mr. Duke.

Don't these guys even care that my ship burned? Hannah thought angrily. I'd think *they* set it on fire, if Hunter, Walt, and I hadn't already caught the real arsonist. "You'll send me a picture when it's done, I hope," she said aloud.

"Sure—be glad to," Mr. Parrish answered. "You and your family will get free riverboat rides on the

General Grant whenever you come to St. Louis."

Big deal, thought Hannah. St. Louis is at least a thousand miles away. Like we're gonna drive over there every week or so. "What're those pylons for?" she asked aloud, pointing to a large circle of yellow plastic cones.

"Keep off—thin ice," explained Mr. Parrish.

"Oh? That's where you pulled the *President Lincoln* up through the ice," Hannah said. "Isn't it already frozen over?"

"Can't take a chance this time o' year," replied Mr. Parrish. "Y'all drive *cars* on the ice here in Maine. Down in Missouri we don't even walk on it. I'm afraid that this late in the winter it may not freeze enough to be safe, even for skating. Before we leave here we're roping this section off and putting up some 'Thin Ice' signs."

※ ※ ※ ※ ※ ※ ※

"Goin' to the Valentine's Day skating party, Walt?" Hannah asked a few days after Mr. Bob Parrish and Mr. Harry Duke left for St. Louis.

"If Papa lets me use the snowmobile, sis. Want to come along?"

"I dunno," Hannah grumped.

Actually, Hannah had asked Walt because one part of her had thought it sounded like fun. She had recently made friends with Sara Melton, whose family had moved to Laketon in the fall. Sara was a bit more than a year older than Hannah, but she was in Hannah's Sunday school class.

"I s'pose I'll go if Sara's going," Hannah replied, hesitating.

Hannah had dragged around lower than Hunter's

basset mother's belly since the *President Lincoln* had gone up in flames. There had been a news conference at Beaver Lodge with a TV camera crew from WABI in Bangor when word got out that Hannah, with Hunter and Walt, had waylaid the crook who set the fire. But Hannah could not bring herself to act like a hero. In fact, she was positively tired of being a celebrity. She had not even thought about the party.

"Sara comin'?" Walt mumbled, embarrassed.

Hannah looked at him out of the corner of her eye, then turned away. "I...I don't know for sure. But I'll phone her."

Sara was one of those girls guys thought were pretty. She was a natural blonde, with delft blue eyes, and her pixie face could pucker into a perfectly round pouty mouth or spread to a wide dimpled smile that could melt snow on Mt. Kineo from several miles away.

Since Sara's parents let their thirteen-year-old daughter use their snowmobile alone as long as she phoned home to say she'd arrived safely, she'd been able to spend an occasional Saturday night with Hannah at Beaver Lodge. Each time, though, Walt had grabbed his shotgun, and with Hunter trotting at his heels or racing ahead, he had left to go rabbit hunting without so much as saying hi to Hannah's guest.

Papa, who understood such matters, called Walt's reaction "chemistry." "Normal guys are often afraid of the girls they really want to like," Hannah overheard him telling Mama in the kitchen one Saturday. "I'd be worried about Walt if he weren't a little scared of a girl as pretty as that."

Keeping her promise to Walt, Hannah phoned Sara on the cellular phone.

"I'll be there," Sara chirped at once. "Daddy's letting me take his snowmobile so Artie can use it to drag some old fence rails out onto the ice—we're goin' t' have a roaring bonfire. Bring a bag o' marshmallows, okay?"

"Sure," Hannah agreed. "Sounds like fun."

Hannah did not digest all that Sara had said until she had hung up the phone. *Artie!* Artie Spearrin was an older boy who lived on Sara's street in Laketon. Hannah had seen him once or twice, and she knew he did not come to church. Still, perhaps it would be all right. Artie seemed like a nice enough guy. But for Sara to have a special friend who did not share her Christian values—this troubled Hannah.

She tried to tell herself that if Artie were going to build the fire, he'd certainly be useful. But Hannah felt bad for Walt.

✻　✻　✻　✻　✻　✻　✻

"Why are we heading out where the steamboat burned?" Hannah yelled at Walt above the roar of the snowmobile's engine.

"'Cause that's where the skating party is." Walt pointed through the snow to a red glow growing larger up ahead. It was a fire, which, because it was snowing lightly, they could not see when they first left Beaver Lodge.

"I thought we were skating in Laketon—at the municipal rink," Hannah protested.

"Can't have a bonfire there."

Without answering, Hannah hunkered down into her parka and clung to Walt, who was driving. Hunter, who had wriggled between brother and sister, kept Hannah's knees warm.

Now Hannah realized why Sara had said they'd need a snowmobile to haul rails for the fire. The Laketon municipal skating rink was a patch of ice on Moosehead Lake next to the village dock. It was kept clear for skating all winter by the village snowplow. But because late-night partygoers had been inconsiderate of other users by building fires in all the wrong places, Laketon's board of selectmen had banned bonfires.

So Sara and Artie had decided to take advantage of the large patch of ice that Mr. Duke and Mr. Parrish had hired a man with a snowplow to clear before raising the President Lincoln.

Hannah had suddenly lost all interest in the Valentine's Day skating party. Her heart ached whenever she remembered the President Lincoln. Now here was another fire where her beloved steamboat had burned to ashes!

Artie Spearrin was busily cutting old cedar fence rails into firewood with a chainsaw when Hannah arrived with Walt and Hunter. Sara was making herself helpful by holding the logs as Artie sawed. Too helpful, Hannah thought.

"Hi, Hannah," Sara called.

"Hi!" Hannah tried to act cheerful. Then she noticed something odd.

"Sara," she asked, as soon as Artie shut off the noisy chainsaw, "the thin spot where the steamboat came up—isn't it supposed to be roped off?"

"We moved the ropes and signs." Sara tossed her blonde curls.

"You guys did *what*?" protested Walt.

"Don't get your dander up," Artie snorted. "I tested the ice myself, an' it's thick enough by now. Best skatin' on the lake, 'cause it's new ice. Smooth as glass."

"Well, if you say so."

"Don't take it so hard, kid." Artie clapped the younger boy on the shoulder. "Your buddies from Missouri just don't know about Maine winters," Artie laughed at Walt. He jerked his thumb toward a tangle of ropes and pylons behind the pile of firewood rails. "That junk was in the way."

Since most of the girls were older than she, Hannah skated by herself most of the evening. Walt, though he enjoyed solo skating, linked arms with Hannah for a few turns around the ice.

Sara, however, had time for Hannah only when Artie was busy adding fuel to the fire.

"You're nervous about the new ice over where they pulled that big boat out, aren't you, Hannah?" Sara asked one of the times she and Hannah skated together.

"Yeah," Hannah admitted, half afraid that Sara would make fun of her just as Artie had teased Walt.

"I don't like it, either," Sara agreed. "It creaks an' groans something awful, but Artie says it's just the cold weather."

Hannah knew that the temperature had risen to the thaw point when they left Beaver Lodge and that the weather report called for the snow to change to a warm rain by midnight, but she didn't disagree with Artie's explanation. "Artie's doing a good job with the fire. Good thing he came along," she answered cheerfully.

Artie skated up just then, and the couple shot away into the darkness.

It happened so fast that later, when the kids at the party explained things to the Maine State Police, no two stories were alike.

Hannah heard Sara scream and Artie holler. She and the others could see just one head—Artie's—above the water. A large sheet of new, thin ice had broken off the old, thick ice, and it tipped to let the skaters slip into the black depths, before sliding back into place.

Walt, who had just removed his skates for the ride home on the snowmobile, grabbed the rope that was supposed to be keeping the skaters off the thin ice. But Artie had left it a useless tangle.

Walt caught up a rail that Artie hadn't yet sawed into firewood. He ran in his stocking feet toward terrified Artie's yells, and Hannah followed with Papa's gas lantern.

And there was Hunter, his teeth sunk into Artie's collar, using his four-paw drive to full advantage to keep the terrified teen from being sucked under by his heavy hockey skates.

"Hang on," Walt yelled. He hauled on the rail and with Hunter's help dragged Artie onto the ice.

Walt then swung the wooden fence rail above his head and brought it down mightily, shattering the floating ice. He peeled off his coat, then dived in.

When Walt surfaced with Sara, he found floating ice cakes in his way as he struggled to reach solid ice. The rail, Hannah discovered, was not long enough to help.

Hunter plunged in and soon came up beside Walt.

Hannah grabbed the rope where Walt had dropped it. "Help me!" she wailed, calling to Artie and several frightened teenagers who had been yelling advice to Walt.

There were knots and tangles everywhere. After what seemed to Hannah an hour, enough of the rope was free to throw. But Walt was now unconscious from hypothermia, his head kept up by Hunter, who was paddling furiously. Sara was out of sight again.

Hannah began to pull the rope in, intending to swim back with it while the others held on. To her surprise, a loop they hadn't untangled fell around Walt's neck, and she easily pulled him over toward the solid ice.

"Let me at him!" The voice of authority was Fire Chief Sylvester, who had responded with his rescue truck when skaters on the municipal rink heard the screams and shouts across the flat ice surface. Chief Sylvester had driven straight onto the ice, and his four-wheel drive had easily taken him through the snow to where Hannah was struggling to pull Walt out by his arms.

❋ ❋ ❋ ❋ ❋ ❋ ❋

"Will Art Spearrin go to jail for illegally removing those barricades?" Walt asked Papa the next evening. The family had been discussing Sara's drowning and what might have been done to prevent it. Hannah, for her part, had found herself unable even to pronounce Artie's name.

"I don't think so. He'll probably get a hefty fine. Maybe a year's probation. What he did was reckless, though I'm not sure it was criminal."

"I expect Artie's learned a far more lasting lesson than any judge could give him," Mama quietly added.

Artie was the only member of the Spearrin family who came to Sara's funeral at Laketon Community Church. After the funeral, several Melton family members and friends lingered at the church to talk. Hannah had wanted to hate Artie, but she found herself thoughtful. After the pink casket was loaded into the black hearse by Walt and three other teen pallbearers, Hannah saw Artie sobbing.

Then Mrs. Melton did something that amazed Hannah. She put both arms around Artie's shoulders, hugged him close, and kissed him on the cheek.

"We love you and we forgive you, Artie." Sara's mom spoke softly through her tears. She seemed to hug as though she never intended to let go, Hannah thought. "You're welcome in our home anytime," Mrs. Melton said sincerely as she released Artie.

"That's right, son. We don't have a boy of our own." It was Mr. Melton speaking as he shook Artie's hand.

With a sorrowful heart Hannah tried to listen as the missionary woman from Africa told of the needs of Masi children in Kenya. It was the Sunday after St. Valentine's Day, and Sara Melton's drowning weighed very heavily indeed in Hannah's thoughts as she listened to this woman, the guest speaker at her Sunday school class in Laketon.

"The Masi," explained Mrs. Abramson, the missionary woman, "are among the world's most primitive people, though they live side by side with other Africans in a rapidly developing country."

Mrs. Abramson then told how education and Bible knowledge would bring light to the dark hearts of those who worship trees and rocks rather than the Living God. Mrs. Abramson showed

Hannah's class a video of colorfully dressed Masi children standing with their parents' herds of cattle. The video also showed these same black children in a school classroom singing songs of praise to Jesus and learning how to read and write.

Hannah heard the woman's words, and she saw the video. But instead of thinking of ways to help, Hannah only sank deeper into her misery. She remembered angrily how her ship, the *President Lincoln*, had burned before she and her friends from St. Louis could proudly put it on display before the entire community. And if she had never even discovered the *President Lincoln*, Hannah thought in dismay, Sara would be alive and sitting beside her in Sunday school class.

When Mrs. Abramson mentioned that a mercy ship carrying doctors and medical supplies and teachers and school equipment would soon sail across the Indian Ocean to East Africa, Hannah's heart was closed. The country of Kenya, in East Africa, with Masi children who needed Jesus, was very, very far away even to think about, Hannah decided.

Chapter Twenty

Dolls for Jesus

Tears blurred Hannah's vision as she added the can of kerosene to her pile of dolls lying face down on the old sled. The sled had been Walt's, then hers, to use for sliding on icy slopes in winter. But this March morning in the snow, Hannah had a sinister use for it, she thought grimly.

Hannah had named her dolls after Jesus' twelve apostles. Now and she could not stand to look at their faces. They had become her dear friends in the months since she had found them in the wreckage of the *President Lincoln*. I can't look at the faces of friends I am about to destroy, Hannah thought bitterly, angry tears rolling down her cheeks.

"You might's well come an' see this, ol' dog," Hannah mourned to Hunter as he danced by her side. She tried to console herself that at least she'd have *one* friend left who'd understand why she had to get rid of her dolls.

"O-o-o-o-o-o-o-oo," Hunter wailed, feeling his mistress's sorrow. He could not possibly know the reason for Hannah's anger and sadness, but he did his best to sympathize.

This early in the morning, the sun had not yet thawed the crust that which had formed overnight on the melting March snow. As Hannah trudged uphill, her boots broke through with each step, scraping her shins raw. But she decided she did not care as she pushed across the pasture behind Papa's barn toward where a big boulder in the old stone wall was swept clean of snow by the warm spring breezes. Here she was determined, before burning her apostles, to smash their china heads.

Hannah rehearsed the events of the past months as she tramped along, and her heart ached as she reviewed each one. She had been so proud to meet the great professor who had discovered the *Titanic*. Then, using clues supplied by him, she had learned that the sunken tug she and Walt had found was really the wreck of the famous steamboat, *President Lincoln*.

Hannah had also become famous. Her picture, as she stood next to the *President Lincoln*, had been in newspapers all across the land. Hannah had even been interviewed on TV.

Hunter, too, was the famous diving dog. Sobbing, Hannah stopped to pet him, scratch his ears, and kiss his wet nose before trudging on.

Then there had been the fire. Hannah's glory had gone up in smoke as Fire Chief Sylvester and the fire department had merely watched it burn, complaining about the mess the burning tires made. Hannah had been robbed of the pleasure of presenting the *President Lincoln* to the people of Laketon, her gift to the folks of her town. What a grand day Hannah had expected that to be!

Even Sheriff Hobson had been cool about her and Hunter and Walt catching the crook who burned the steamboat. What did he care about the *President Lincoln*? As for Mr. Duke and Mr. Parrish, they had taken a plane back to St. Louis to finish restoring the *General Grant*. Though they had lost a lot of money, certainly, they seemed glad to merely leave Maine without losing more. To them, it was as though there had never been a *President Lincoln*.

Hannah just then really and truly wished that the *President Lincoln* had never been found.

Hannah hurt terribly when she remembered the St. Valentine's drowning. A girl Hannah had just begun to be friends with had gone through the thin ice right where Mr. Duke and Mr. Parrish had pulled the President Lincoln up from the lake bottom.

"Sara Melton would be alive today if I hadn't found that ol' boat," Hannah told Hunter in despair.

So this had to be. If I hadn't been so proud, I'd not be in this mess. Even the dolls, Hannah remembered sadly, had been famous. They even had their pictures taken for an article that appeared in *The Saturday Evening Post*. The dolls, her twelve apostles, were all Hannah had left to be proud of. And wasn't it pride that had caused Hannah so much trouble? With the dolls destroyed, she thought grimly, her pride would be gone forever.

Hannah carefully piled the dolls in a heap beside the big rock. She fingered the matches in her pocket. With all this snow still on the ground, she decided, there was no danger of setting the woods on fire.

Slowly she unscrewed the cap on the kerosene can, sadly considering all the fine needlework she and Mama had put into sewing those doll dresses. And the cloth and sawdust bodies? Papa had lovingly spent several evenings making them for his daughter. But the heads, hands, and feet were the real antiques, 150 years old, bought in China.

What am I thinking? Hannah set the kerosene can down. Smash the heads first. That was my plan. I don't want to dig them out of the ashes later, like Mr. Duke and Mr. Parrish had to do to get enough bolts to finish restoring the General Grant.

She grabbed up Judith Iscariot. Good choice. Judas was the traitor. Hannah took careful aim at the boulder. Closing her eyes and sucking in her breath, Hannah threw with all her might.

"Plunk." Hannah had expected a "pop" from smashing china. She peeked. No Judith. At her feet, Hunter wagged his tail and rolled his brown eyes up in expectation. In his soft hound mouth he lovingly held Judith, unharmed. It dawned on Hannah at that moment that her dolls really belonged to the Lord—everything belonged to the Lord.

Hannah sat sobbing on the sled beside the precious, beloved dolls. She sobbed and she sobbed and she sobbed. Then with her toe, Hannah tipped over the kerosene can and let the fuel run out into the snow. Mama didn't use it anymore, now that Beaver Lodge had electric lights.

Hannah suddenly remembered the Bible's Hannah, after whom she—Hannah Parmenter—had been named. This godly woman had borne a son, for whom she had earnestly prayed. Yet Hannah of old, to keep her promise to God, had handed her son Samuel back to God while he was still a child.

Hannah laughed through her tears, remembering how the other Hannah had celebrated God's praises in song. The Bible's Hannah had found it a privilege to return to God what God had given her. But one cannot return what one has destroyed. How glad Hannah was that God had put it in Hunter's silly hound head to rescue Apostle Judith!

Hugging Judith with one arm and Hunter with the other, Hannah cried some more.

"Hunter, sometimes you're wiser than I am," she said at last.

"R-r-r-uff!" Hunter agreed.

"Hannah, why have you been taking your dolls for a sled ride?" Mama asked moments later, as Hannah stomped the snow off her boots on the entry mat.

"I...I'm not sure you'd understand."

"Try me."

Mama kissed Hannah's forehead, then picked up several of the dolls and helped Hannah carry them up to her room.

"Mama," Hannah said once they were upstairs in her bedroom. "When you're proud, why doesn't it help to destroy what you're proud of?"

Hannah thought she knew the answer, but Mama always gave such thoughtful answers that she had to ask.

"Would it have helped if Adam and Eve had cut down the tree?" Mama asked.

"I...I don't suppose it would have."

"Why did Eve eat the forbidden fruit?" Mama asked quietly.

"Well, the Bible says that Satan the snake promised her that it would make her like God. I guess that's pride, isn't it?"

"You're very perceptive," Mama noted.

"And since pride is a sin of the heart, getting rid of what you're proud of won't help," Hannah thoughtfully added.

"Sometimes it may seem to help, I suppose," Mama said. "But it doesn't solve the real, root problem, does it?"

Mama carefully patted the dolls' dresses, smoothing them down as she spoke.

"You know, Mama," Hannah brightened. "When I asked Jesus into my heart, that was spiritual.

Destroying the dolls is physical, and it can't help a spiritual problem, like pride—isn't that what Paul teaches in the book of Galatians?"

"It surely is," Mama agreed.

"I thank you, Lord, for all the good and wonderful things that have happened to me," Hannah prayed, kneeling beside her bed as soon as Mama had gone downstairs. "I even thank you for letting the *President Lincoln* burn. It taught me that everything I wish to treasure has got t' go, sooner or later. I've learned that I've got to trust You for everything I need.

"Even for losing my friend Sara, I thank You, Jesus, though I don't understand why You took her. Forgive my anger at the twelve apostles, which was really being mad at You for not letting me have my own proud, selfish way. And please help Sara's parents in their grief. In Jesus' name. Amen."

When Walt brought the week's mail from Laketon on the snowmobile that afternoon, there were two letters for Hannah. The curator of America's famous national museum, the Smithsonian Institution in Washington, D.C., had written to say that he'd seen Hannah's unusual collection of dolls in the *Post* article. The museum needed such a marvelous collection from the old days of trading with China by sailing ship, he had explained. If Hannah would consider selling them, the Smithsonian would even send an expert to appraise their value. She could expect to be paid well for the dolls, the curator had said.

The other letter was from Mrs. Abramson, the woman missionary who had spoken to Hannah's Sunday school class about a month ago, right after

Sara Melton had drowned on Valentine's Day. Mrs. Abramson's mission needed to finish loading a mercy ship to carry books and supplies for a school in Kenya, Africa. These materials would give a Christian education to Masi children, a primitive tribe living in a nation that is rapidly being modernized.

Though the missionary had shown a video of happy Masi children singing God's praises and learning to read the Bible, Hannah in her misery and sorrow had tried hard to ignore the lesson. But God was speaking to her, all the same.

I have a choice much like Eve's choice, Hannah thought, her head swimming with the meaning of both letters. Hannah recalled from reading the creation story in her Bible that Eve could have chosen to obey God. Instead, she ate the fruit, proudly choosing to try to be like God, as the serpent had promised. Eve, Hannah knew, had made the wrong choice, which had brought her only shame and misery.

"Apostles, you are going to heaven," Hannah said at last, laughing as she eyed her twelve china dolls. The teaching of Jesus to "lay up your treasures in heaven" by giving to meet the needs of others came into her head at that moment. It touched Hannah's heart, as well.

"If I sell you guys, then give the money so Masi kids can learn to read the Bible and learn about Jesus, that's laying my treasure up in heaven, isn't it?" Hannah asked. "God has given me much happiness in owning you. It's time you dolls made someone else happy."

The silent dolls did not answer. But Hannah knew the truth.